STARCROSSED

Corinne's story
continues in...

Ascended

[coming soon]

ALSO BY KATIE JANE GALLAGHER

The Gold in the Dark
(free at katiejgallagher.com)

Specter

Beauty and Her Alien series

Unearthly
Starcrossed

HIDDEN
BOWER

Printed and bound in the United States of America.

All characters appearing in this work are fictitious. Any resemblance to real persons, living or dead, is purely coincidental.

ISBN: 978-1-7377895-1-2

First Edition First Printing
Cover Illustration Copyright © 2021 by LianaM.
Old Retro Labels TFB font by zanatlija.
Sexything font by Xavier Puig.
Optimus Princeps font by Manfred Klein.
Beauty and the Beast quote from Master Charles Perault's *Old-Time Stories*.

www.katiejgallagher.com

For every person who has ever longed for

their very own beast.

STARCROSSED

KATIE JANE GALLAGHER

HIDDEN
BOWER

BOOK

Two

*'Oh yes,' answered the Beast, 'I have a good
heart, right enough, but I am a monster.'*

*'There are many men,' said Beauty, 'who make
worse monsters than you, and I prefer you to
those who under the semblance of men hide
false, corrupt, and ungrateful hearts.'*

Chapter One

I WAS SITTING CROSS-LEGGED AT THE FOOT OF MY BIG, BEAUTIFUL bed in my big, beautiful room in my big, beautiful alien spaceship, and I was feeling pretty miffed.

Joanna made a small noise of frustration. "And you're sure you wouldn't like me to give you a rundown…?" If she'd had hands, she'd have been wringing them. Joanna, however, is a being not of flesh and blood, but an amorphous AI who floats about the ship at will, displaying on the walls as a heap of shifting fractals. Right now her fractals were a bright aquamarine that meant, *I'm upset*.

That made two of us.

"We can talk about the sister later," I said. I'm sorry to say that my irritation was present in my tone. Normally I am adept at keeping a lid on my emotions when I'd like—years of customer service will do that to a person. But this wasn't any sort of a normal time. I had just kissed the owner of this spaceship, who was not a human but a rumae, and a rumae *prince* at that. Lots to think about there—most of it good.

What I didn't like was being right in the middle of said kissing, which, again, had been good—very, very good—really quite excellent—only for Joanna to cut in, bearing bad news. Jexrah, Del's sister, was boarding the ship, and she was purportedly frightful.

So now I'd been sent to my room like a naughty toddler, and coming down from the high of the sim-room events had me aching all over, and thinking about Del, and who he was, and what had happened, and what *might* have happened… well, all of that lumped together was a lot to process, and what I wanted was a little more time to *think*, without Joanna interrup—

"His sister is on her way over," Joanna said, her blue going fluorescent. "She'll be here momentarily. Maybe put Midge in the other room?" Midge, my dog and fellow abductee, was currently seated next to me on the bed, looking at me worriedly. She's smart, a black, medium-haired mutt, and if I was about to meet the awful sister, then I wanted her beside me.

"I can handle Jexrah," I snapped, "and I'm sure she can handle my dog!" How bad could the princess be?

Hindsight's twenty-twenty, they say.

The sister burst into my suite yammering in Ziryahshun to a silvery little drone that buzzed like an oversized mosquito, its flight pattern slightly tipsy. At Jexrah's heel was one of the server bots, its appendages straining to carry several bulky pieces of luggage.

Jexrah stopped dead when she saw me, and the drone did an excited little loop-de-loop. There were a few dismayed beeps from the overladen server bot as it put on the brakes, just managing to avoid a rear-end collision with the alien princess. Then it performed a deferential shuffle toward the wall and stilled, as if anticipating a long conversation. Meanwhile, Midge had gone rigid, her eyes fixed on the drone, and I swooped her up into my arms as she poised to spring.

I had miscalculated this encounter.

Jexrah and I shared a look at each other as Midge tried to wriggle free. If Del's sister was anything to go by, female rumae were smaller than their male counterparts, but not by much; she had a good five inches on me at least. She had Del's same red eyes, but that's where the similarities ended. Rather than his reddish coloring, Jexrah's fur was a black-and-brown patchwork, tortoiseshell cat-like. (I made a mental note to have Joanna conjure me up a book on rumae anatomy and physiology—because seeing Jexrah had gotten me curious. I had no *other* reason for such a book.)

Every part of Jexrah's look screamed feminine power, from the intricate patterns carved into her long, dark nails to the puffy swell of her mane. The eighties must still be in on Tenctah; I squinted at her hair, wondering if she'd teased it or if all that volume came naturally. Clothing-wise, she was clad in a tight, black, strappy get-up that was more holes than fabric, leaving most of her lean musculature on full display. I guess if you have fur, clothing coverage is more of an afterthought. After hustling back from Del's sim room, I'd wiped off the gold-dust nanotech and changed back into leggings and a T-shirt, but I doubt Jexrah would have blinked at my sim-room bikini.

"Hello," I said, forgetting my elementary Ziryahshun. Well, let's be honest: I didn't feel much draw to use it with her anyway, alien princess notwithstanding. She wasn't *my* princess, and, more importantly, she seemed like trouble. We were going to stick with English.

"Interesting," she said after she'd gotten a good look at me. Her English was accented, but perfectly understandable, her voice cool. "I'd heard one of you was aboard." Charming. "And what are you doing in my suite?"

Her suite? And then I remembered the settings of the room's mirror when I'd first arrived, how they'd been set to full glamour.

"I live here," I said simply.

"Interesting," she said again, red eyes glittering as she considered me. Then the drone made a drunken dive-bomb maneuver in Midge's direction, and I fell back a step. Midge gave a warning bark, her every muscle tense. This was going well.

"Oh, stop it," Jexrah said. "We wouldn't want to scare the pet." God, I hoped she was talking about Midge. "My older sister, Khindrae Lizgamyarah Sharbrit Meervit, by the way," she said, flicking one of those wickedly long nails at the drone. "She's just along for the ride."

"Pleased," I said with a forced smile and a nod at something-something-something-Meervit. The drone was giving me the oddest feeling of déjà vu. How many sisters did Del have, and were any of the rest of them mechanical?

Meervit buzzed a few squeaky words in Ziryahshun, and Jexrah chortled something in response. I kept my smile on, all while my insides squirmed. I was getting that distinctive middle-school feeling where you know the girls just a few feet out of earshot are talking about you.

"My dear sister's on the planet," Jexrah told me, switching back to English. "So do forgive her if she flies a bit off-balance. The connection always takes time to settle in after the snap travel." She punctuated this with a bright smile that said, *that explains it all, doesn't it?* Like her brother, she had many sharp white teeth.

"Ah, right. Great." I adjusted my grip on Midge; she was heavy to hold for this long, but I couldn't risk her biting royalty.

"So!" Jexrah continued with a glance around. "It's a nice space, isn't it?"

"Sure." One-syllable words were all I seemed to be able to manage for the time being.

She regarded me for another interminable moment. "It shows high esteem that my brother offered to let you stay in this area of the ship. Myself, I've never found the other guest suites on my brother's ship to quite match the opulence of these quarters." Then she gave me another one of *those looks*, the kind where you're clearly supposed to say *that obvious thing*.

"I'm very happy Del allows me to stay here," I said slowly, feeling very much like a kid who's gotten called on out of the blue in class.

"Del!" Jexrah said, eyes widening slightly. "Well then!" The drone had been cruising about the room for the past minute, but now it buzzed in a wobbly flight path back to us before about-facing toward the door, babbling a tinny stream of Ziryahshun the whole time. Too bad the drone cops weren't here to give her a DUI. They're never around when you need them.

"I suppose you're correct," Jexrah said to her sister, in English this time. "Different customs and all that." Again I thought of those middle-school girls—the evil ones who not only are talking about you, but want you to know about it.

Jexrah's attention swung back to me. "Well, this has been an enlightening conversation. I anticipate we'll have the pleasure of getting to know each other better soon. In the meantime, duty awaits." She fluttered a hand toward the door, her mane bobbing. "*Del*. You understand, of course."

And with that last mystifying statement she swept away with her drone in tow, the server bot trundling along behind them. Midge gave a little growl as they left, and I hugged her in closer before letting her down to the ground.

"Joanna," I called out as soon as the door closed. I'd seen wisps of her usual apricot at the edges of the room throughout the whole bizarre conversation. "I need you."

"I'm here," she said as her fractals faded in. I'd never been so happy to hear her familiar British tones.

"I need a breakdown. She wants something from me, but I don't speak alien princess."

Joanna's orange grew darker. "She was testing you. She was indicating you should give up your quarters to her. Any Ailoptian would, out of respect. Not that the khindrae much cares, I'm sure—she just wanted to get a sense of your feelings toward her, as royalty. Or lack thereof."

Well, that was one mystery solved—and a test I had failed

with flying colors. "What else? What was all that she was saying about the sister being on the planet?"

"Khindrae Meervit's physical body is at her estate on Tenctah. The khindrae unfortunately suffers from a disease that makes physical movement quite painful, so she's come to enjoy spending the majority of her waking hours in drone form. She's well-known for having many such drones crafted to her exact specifications installed throughout the residences of the royal family and its associates, to allow her to come and go as the khindrae pleases. Long-distance space travel can cause a certain amount of communication lag, though, hence the erratic movements."

That meant I could give the sister, at least, the benefit of the doubt; she might not have been purposefully antagonizing my dog. "And *khindrae* means princess? Lady? Something like that?"

"Correct," said Joanna. "Khindrae Morgvimah Sharbrit Jexrah and Khindrae Lizgamyarah Sharbrit Meervit—Khindrae Jexrah and Khindrae Meervit in common parlance. Vra-khinahar Delklor—you know that one. There's a lot of official terminology. We could do a little lesson on all the terms, if you'd like."

"Later," I said, reaching for Midge's ball. She deserved some playtime after all the commotion with the drone—what *was* it about Meervit that felt so familiar?—and I could use some zoning-out time to think about… all that had happened. Not just about right here, right now, but also about what had happened in the simulation room…

Yet Joanna's words gave me a sudden thought. *Vra-khinahar Delklor… official terminology…*

"There's not something… *inappropriate* about calling Del, well, Del—is there? Just a few things Jexrah said…"

Joanna's geometries made an uncomfortable little squirm. "That's the way the master introduced himself to you. Whatever appellation he conveyed to you would be the most appropriate choice, naturally."

The master this, the master that—always such formality. None of what she was saying was putting me at ease. "Naturally," I agreed. "But would you say it might raise eyebrows from other rumae? Like, if, er, Mr. Darcy were here, and I called him Fitz…"

She squirmed a little more. "There is some comparison to be made. It would imply to others that you are both quite familiar with each other."

Great. Lord knew what Jexrah thought about that—hopefully that I was just some human yokel without an understanding of the word *propriety*. But it didn't seem like something the so-called "scheming busybody" would overlook. I was increasingly feeling like I hadn't been set up for success in dealing with Del's sister.

Which said to me that the best plan was to make myself scarce. It had not escaped me that I'd just put myself in a rather delicate political situation by kissing the heir to the throne of an alien nation of over two billion people. So if Jexrah wanted to go sniffing about the ship, fine. I was just the hapless, etiquette-obtuse prisoner. Nothing to see here!

"Here's what I need," I said slowly, pacing the room. "Can you set me a… a princess watch or something like that? Keep tabs on Jexrah's movements. And Meervit, if she decides to stick around. The goal is avoidance. If it seems like they want to come talk to me, I'm preoccupied—sick, sleeping, taking a bath… whatever sounds best."

"Consider it done."

Wonderful. And now that I had mentioned taking a bath, I found that my bathtub was calling to me—the one fit for royalty, I thought with a grim smile as I went to draw the water. I would make sure to enjoy it, princess though I might not be. Hah! And then, after that, a night in sounded just about perfect, to counterbalance today's val hunt and the—everything else that had happened today. So I would have a quiet night in—fabricate some nail polish and give myself a manicure, maybe a face mask as well, an episode of something fun to watch…

The bath was just getting all nice and bubbly when Joanna cut in. "Khindrae Jexrah is requesting the honor of your presence tomorrow morning at eleven o'clock. She proposes some light refreshments on the top deck—just yourself and the khindrae. Will you accept?"

I gritted my teeth; I hadn't factored this sort of thing into my princess plan. "Tell her yes," I said after a moment, then sank back into my bath with a sigh. Problem solved: I was a human woman in her twenties, and I knew how these things worked.

Yes to whatever stupid plans the khindrae proposed—why the hell not? Yes—with every intention to cancel.

Chapter Two

THE NEXT DAY I WOKE UP LATE AND LAZED THROUGH MY MORNING routine, the eleven o'clock deadline like a slowly tightening noose around my neck. Fifteen minutes till, Joanna gave me a soft reminder of the approaching meeting. Ten minutes till, she expressed to me that wearing yesterday's leggings and a T-shirt with a dirt stain might not be an appropriate outfit for a meeting with the khindrae; nodding, I let her fabricate me another pair of Lululemons and a soft coral tee. At three minutes till, her usual apricot now limned with deep, worried blue, Joanna asked if it might be a good idea to get going.

"Right," I said, slipping on my shoes. "Please give the khindrae my sincerest apologies. I have a terrible migraine coming on, and the light on the top deck would make it ten times worse."

"But you've already accepted her invitation!" she said, twisting herself into nervous navy knots. *She's up there waiting for you.* It would be the height of rudeness to—"

But I was already striding out the door, headed for the hot-house. I let Midge stay behind; she didn't need to be part of whatever might come next.

I'd decided to turn my attentions to beating back some of the wildness of the hothouse. There was a lot of work to do: uprooting the toxic tuahdes, skimming the algae sludge from the surface of the pool beside the gazebo, finding higher resting places for the vines that swung low over the path. Small touches to help the hothouse's raw beauty shine.

I started a mental count of the minutes in my head and turned my attention to a shrub called a *voh rabinnut*, so Joanna told me. It had shed many of its conical, lavender-colored flow-ers in recent days; here was my opportunity to see if deadhead-ing was an Earth-specific phenomenon, or if it had some effect on Tenctah's flora, too. I snapped off the ends of each newly bare flower stem, then took some quick notes in my sketch-book; I'd compare this bush with another one across the way and see if I could get more flowers.

How long had it taken to deadhead the shrub—ten minutes or thereabouts? Hm. I glanced down the path in both direc-tions, smiled, then pressed on.

Next on the agenda was an overgrown little grove that looked like it could do with some weeding. Hopefully the spiky little plants choking out the rest of the area were actually weeds and not some more precious species... I had a sudden vision of unwittingly ripping out million-dollar plants to make room for Tenctah's version of a dandelion.

Oh well, who cared? It seemed like I was going to be the only person who ever came in here anyway. I shook off my doubts and grasped the base of the first stem.

"Good morning," called a voice cheerily from behind me.

I closed my eyes for a moment, then opened them and rose to my feet, ripping up the plant with a snapping of roots. They dangled below the stem like thin, red entrails.

It was Jexrah, of course, dressed today in another outfit that looked suited for BDSM play: yet more straps, jade green this time. Each strap came adorned with bits of sculpted fabric that jutted out, pufferfish-like, to stab at the air.

"Morning," I answered.

"You have a headache, I hear."

"I do." I mean, *now* I had one coming on.

We surveyed each other coolly, her with clear doubt, me with an expression that I hoped conveyed something like, *Well, what are you going to do about it—ask for a doctor's note? Stab me to death with your fabric knives?*

"Water and proper sustenance should be of help," she said. *Proper sustenance*—you couldn't tell she was Del's sister, could you? She waved a hand around us vaguely. "I can't imagine it's a help to be laboring in this heat."

"Heat and humidity are common human remedies for headaches and migraines," I lied, forcing a smile. "I really would love to eat with you… get to know each other… But—"

"Oh, of course," she said, the very picture of grace. "That's why I sent a server bot to fetch the food from upstairs. Share a meal with me, won't you? Rest a bit. I'm eager to learn more about the person who's been living alongside my dear brother this past while."

Well, dammit. My first hope had been that she'd let me get away with my obviously bullshit excuse. My second hope had been that she'd venture down here and I'd be able to ward her off with a bit more bullshit.

But I was clearly outclassed. And, I realized with a sinking feeling as I trudged after the khindrae back to the gazebo, *and* I was having a difficult time recalling all the inane social rules about who was supposed to eat what when.

Smack-dab in the middle of the gazebo now sat a low table and two chairs; the server bots worked fast. The table was clustered with various delicacies, along with two sweating glasses of water.

Taking off my gardening gloves, I balled them up and tossed them to the side of the gazebo with a bit more force than was strictly necessary. Then, sitting down, I gritted my teeth and pasted a smile over them that I hoped looked pleasant. I was sure it did not.

"How considerate of you to bring all this down here."

"My pleasure. Oh, here," she said, swooping in with her fork to grab the first bite. Well, that satisfied that question. Of course she got to have first-bite honors: she was *Jexrah*, after all, and I just the lowly human, scarcely better than dirt. I made a quick decision not to do the whole share-food-around thing; if she called me out, I'd feign alien ignorance.

"Dig in," she said, looking at me from across the table with a smug smile. I picked a little at this dish and that—it was your standard strange rumae fare. Thankfully there was a dish of my favorite pickled red almost-carrots near me, to which I turned most of my attention.

"You enjoy Ailoptian cuisine," Jexrah observed.

"I enjoy these," I said, jabbing at the almost-carrots with my fork.

"*Axhlot.* They are called axhlot. And how have you found the rest of your stay aboard? Agreeable, I hope?"

"It's a very nice prison, yes." Oh dear, that was probably the sort of thing I wasn't supposed to say to the khindrae. Jexrah straightened up in her seat with a look that said *oh-ho!*

"So you'd prefer that you were back home, then," she said, taking a small bite of something all while keeping her eyes on me.

"Yes…"

"I see," she said, reaching across the table for a square of a lumpy, dried brown paste. I followed her lead and nibbled at a corner; it had a subtle, tea-like taste. Not bad, really. "I am gladdened to see, though," she continued, "that despite your confinement here you have found ways to occupy yourself." She waved a hand through the air at the space around us. "It's good to have pastimes. They will be a comfort to you once the ship departs your planet at last."

She *was* nice to talk with, wasn't she? "I suppose," I said tightly, reaching for my water. Then a sudden paranoia hit me; could she have dosed the water with some sort of alien truth serum? I had no idea the lengths she'd go to get information; after all, we were here alone, away from any supervision by Joanna. I brushed a fingertip against the glass, drawing an *F* and then a *U* in the beaded condensation.

"So what brings you to the *Huivnarrut?*" I asked, deciding to flip the tables and pose a few questions of my own.

"*H—?*" Blink and you'd miss it: something about the question had smashed through her practiced smarminess for a fraction of a second. Perhaps my terrible pronunciation of the ship's new name. "You might say I'm just checking in. Oh, my brother *has* informed you about the circumstances preceding his temporary presence on Earth, hasn't he?"

"No, he hasn't," I admitted.

She looked decidedly pleased. "Oh. Well, no matter. Here, you must try this—one of my favorites." She pointed at a dish heaped full of what looked like gray soft-serve ice cream, unnervingly solid for this heat. I waited until she went for the first bite before sampling any of the gray stuff myself. Sweet, with a slight lemony flavor—aside from a faint, oily aftertaste, it was pretty good.

"Mm."

Jexrah gave a proud nod. "Ailoptian cuisine is second to none. Would you tell me how you came to be on the ship? It must have been quite a shock."

A chill fell over me, despite the heat. What did she already know? One wrong word could put my dad in danger; after all, he wasn't supposed to have left the ship.

"I was out walking in the woods. I was being careless, and there was a snowstorm… I got lost and happened upon the *Huivnarrut.*" Her eyes narrowed a hair again; she definitely hadn't known about the name change. "And so… here I am," I said, spreading my arms. Best to keep my story simple and as close to the facts as possible.

"Yes," Jexrah said slowly, as my nerves crawled. "Here you

are." She reached for her water. Took a sip and set the glass back down. Then she looked me dead in the eye.

"Everyone has their faults," she said. "Myself, I've always been excessively curious. Growing up I was an annoyance to my family and peers—always asking questions, digging into places where I wasn't wanted. There were a few times in my more naive years when I unearthed information to cause a scandal. Love affairs... a quiet assassination by poison... that sort of thing. I've since learned to keep my secrets close.

"Last night I found myself unable to fall asleep for some time. Snap travel has that tendency... or perhaps it was the novelty of the unfamiliar suite. Anyway, I'll admit that in my insomniac state I gave into my vice: I did a bit of digging.

"You, Corinne Kaminski, are seemingly a nobody. Though you live in what seems by all accounts to be the most powerful country on your planet, your so-called state of 'Montana' appears largely to keep to itself, not figuring in much to the national narrative. Your father works an ordinary job, as did you. Records indicate that your social standing is average. You are, by all indications, of the common people—an upstanding member of society, no doubt, but someone who hasn't made much of a mark on the world. Well, you're still young for your species; you have time yet.

"And, as you related, it was an inexplicable accident that led to you coming aboard the... *Huivnarrut*. I believe that fact wholeheartedly; you're simply too ordinary for it to have happened any other way.

"And yet the circumstances surrounding you once you

boarded the ship are bizarre. Per my personal steward's analysis, there's about a seventy-percent chance that the security footage of your first day on board has been doctored, as well as that of the following day—oh yes, I took a peek at that, despite my brother's steward's protestations. The weight of my rank simply made the request undeniable. Do you know, my steward actually suggested that someone had put in some considerable work ensuring your arrival time on the security footage corresponded with your entry time on the Intelligent Alien Species Registry!

"Strange, too, that there was no DNA sample taken during the first hour of your arrival, as is best practice. That sample was submitted to the registry the day following your recorded arrival time." She gave me a grim little smile. "Odd, isn't it?"

"Very odd," I said numbly.

"And," she continued, "there have been other such security footage irregularities in the days following. These irregularities persist even up to the minutes before my boarding. If you recall, yesterday you came here to the hothouse and spent more than an hour inside. Doing what, I'm uncertain—I'm sure you haven't realized this, but this space affords those within a great deal of privacy. A severe security oversight—I've made sure to voice my concerns about that with my brother.

"After your time gardening… or whatever you were doing… you returned to your suite, changed your outfit, and then met my brother in his sim room. Everything proceeds normally for some time, then—again, this is just what has been suggested per my steward's analysis—the security footage once more exhibits slight indications of being doctored!" She sat back in her seat, red eyes gleaming. "Isn't that incredible?"

"I've been told the ship has been undergoing some repairs," I said, tongue dry. "Maybe the security footage has been affected."

She reached across the table and speared a piece of axhlot with her claw, the point punching through it with a loud crunch. I'm sorry to say I flinched. "Of course—that's precisely what his steward told me. All this amounts to nothing, I'm sure.

"But I will say I have a *feeling* about you, Corinne Kaminski. And here, away from the eyes and ears of my brother's loyal ship steward, I'll be forthright: I think you're up to something. I don't know what, or how, or why... but when the vrakhinahar is involved, these vague hunches do count for something." She took a bite of the axhlot and made an approving sound. "These *are* quite good. And how refreshing to sit here in privacy and speak candidly with you! Your refusal to dine with me upstairs turned out well in the end, didn't it?"

I was too aghast to respond, and there was no doubt that she knew it.

"Well," she said, after a second's silence, "this has been pleasant. Let's leave the matter here. Maybe you and I can have another chat sometime soon." Then she got up from her chair and left me alone with just my host of worries for company.

Chapter Three

I SPENT THE NEXT FEW HOURS HOLED UP IN MY ROOM IN A SOUR, anxious mood. To my great relief, Joanna didn't probe me on the unpleasantries between myself and Jexrah in the hothouse. I'm sure she was curious, and not just because her role as ship steward demanded it, but she was also tactful enough to let it lie, for now.

I tried to drown my fears with distractions. I watched an episode I'd been meaning to get to. I did a session of yoga on the floor, with a newly fabricated mat. I dove back into the latest in my mystery series, this one just as bad as the last. Nothing helped; Jexrah's words were a constant echo in my mind.

"What does *Huivnarrut* really mean?" I asked Joanna, setting the book down with a sigh. It was all too obvious who the killer was. It was also all too obvious that Joanna hadn't been entirely honest with me that the ship's moniker was just some untranslatable, poetic word.

Her fractals grew sluggish, the tips lightening to pastel.

"Be honest," I said. "Please."

"It… it *is* a turn of phrase that's difficult to translate."

"Try."

When she answered, her words were slow and hesitating. I'd never heard her sound so deeply uncomfortable. "It's a melancholy word. Something like… 'disappointment.' But with more depth than that. There's a sense of not having met obligations to one's family or community. That the person in question appeared to be… upstanding. But now has been revealed as something of a—a charlatan. It is an unsettling name for a ship."

What she meant was that it was an inappropriate name—but of course Joanna was too loyal to her master to voice such sentiments. It was more and more clear that there was something like a sickness on board the ship. Something hidden and unspoken… Something wrong.

I shook my head, flummoxed. "Why would Del rename the ship like that?"

Her shifting geometries had slowed to a molasses-like crawl. "I'm so, so sorry, but—"

"—you can't tell me that," I said, nodding. "All right. No, I'm not going to throw anything at you. I'd—I'd pinkie swear with you if I could." The way she was coiling read as distinctly worried, and I was very sorry for it. We'd had our tense moments, me and Joanna, but now that Jexrah was in the picture I needed every ally I could muster.

"Can you tell me *why* she didn't know about the name change?" I asked.

"Oh, that. I… never formally put in the request. Haven't done so yet, I should say."

"Naughty. You hate the name."

"One is allowed a certain amount of time after ship repairs are completed to register a new name," she said primly. "And we're not yet finished with the repairs."

"You're hoping he'll change his mind."

"I am… allowing him the opportunity to do so, if he chooses. A royal steward must keep these possibilities in mind."

Sure, sure. "Is Del eating dinner with his sister tonight?" I asked.

"Sisters. Khindrae Meervit has decided to dine with them as well."

I shuddered as I pictured Del and Jexrah verbally sparring over dinner, while Meervit buzzed in loopy circles around the table. That was a family scene I wanted no part of. Though I did long to see Del again—and not just so I could confirm to him that Jexrah was, in fact, "the worst of them all," as he'd put it. But just… to see him. And the kiss—that was never far from my mind.

But how could I think like that, when getting home was the most important thing? Escaping the ship had to remain my first priority.

"We could get back to *Emma*," Joanna suggested, bringing me back to the present.

"I'm not feeling it."

"You could finish your book, then?" she said, meaning my tedious mystery.

"I figured it out already. The grandfather's old business partner is the killer. He resented how the grandfather gifted Fran all that money to open her bakery." Joanna liked it when I gave her the blow-by-blow.

"What about your theory that it was the philanthropist widow?"

"That whole part was a red herring," I said woefully. "The only reason I can figure out that she's in the book is to tell us more of Wes's backstory."

"That's the hunky cop love interest?"

"Right. Anyway, I think I'm done with it," I said, wrinkling my nose at the hundred pages I still had left.

"How about I write you a book with a better plot?"

"You could do that?"

Her usual orange took on a golden gleam. "Corinne... I don't want to boast, but I have at my disposal the entire breadth of human knowledge when it comes to literature, storytelling, and creative theory. I'm certain I can generate something that will prove more entertaining to you. Or..." She paused. "There is something else I could make for you."

I was still struggling to come to terms with the notion that Joanna seemed to think she had the capability of writing a bestseller at the drop of a hat. And that maybe she was right. "W-what else?"

"I would have to show you. But it's in another part of the ship."

I grimaced, loathe to leave my room and risk bumping into any stray alien royalty. "Any updates on the princess watch?"

"Khindrae Jexrah is sprucing up in her room. Her sister is with her. In my estimation, she will not seek you out again until at least tomorrow morning, if not later. I believe she's planning some sort of recreational activity for you, herself, and the master to all enjoy together."

Splendid. "Like minigolf or something?"

She chuckled. "Doubtful—minigolf is a purely human phenomenon. The khindrae isn't letting me be privy to the details, unfortunately."

"Well," I said, standing up and stretching, "I'm up for a field trip. Lead on."

She brought me to a small, dark room down the hall. The furniture arrangement was odd: a sort of low, circular couch took up most of the space, in the middle of which was…

"Oh," I said softly, now seeing the room's contents with new eyes. I'd poked my head in here before, during my earlier explorations of the ship, but hadn't known what I was looking at. Now I recognized the hunk of machinery in the center of the room as a larger version of the techy cauldron downstairs in Del's quarters.

"The rumae use it partly as an entertainment system," Joanna explained as I took a seat on the couch. The cauldron's top retracted; this time the mist within was a neutral white. "Think of it like a TV/video-game hybrid. So you might have your female super sleuth…" The mist bloomed with color as it coalesced into the shape of a woman's body, standing about five inches high. "We'll call her…"

"Nadia," I supplied off the top of my head.

"Right," said Joanna. "Nadia." And sure enough, the mist shifted, changed, deepened, until the character before me was downright imbued with Nadia-ness. The planes of her face were sharp but beautiful, her cool blue eyes observant, her dark hair cut into a precise lob that just brushed her shoulders.

"As best I can tell," Joanna said, "humans have a sort of murky collective consciousness when it comes to names. This seems to me like what a Nadia should look like. Do you agree?"

"Yeah." There was no denying it.

"So then we can pick a setting for her. What would you say? Rural Alaska? Vacation town in Maine? Suburb of Chicago?"

"S-sure. That last one sounds good."

"Excellent. And we'll have a kooky but lovable cast of characters to surround her. A love interest, of course. Or maybe a few, so we can pick one along the way?"

"The more the merrier," I said faintly.

"Did you have any sort of backstory in mind for our Nadia?"

"Whatever you think works best."

"Perfect," she said. "And then off you go—let's solve a mystery, shall we?" Out of the mist, a setting melted in around Nadia—a small but tastefully decorated bedroom—and Joanna's voice shifted into a theatrical register as she began describing our heroine. Meanwhile, Nadia was tidying up—dusting a few family photos on top of her dresser, emptying the trash can in the corner, fluffing the pillows on her bed. As it turned out, Nadia was a professional organizer with a biting wit that would have set Marie Kondo and her thank-the-house spiritualism running. We next followed her to a job where she discovered a dead body smack-dab in the middle of the messy garage she was supposed to be tackling that day, and, true to form, she was soon surrounded by the oddball cast Joanna had promised.

A couple hours in, I was stumped and in need of more clues, Nadia was at a bar trying to flirt a key piece of information out of the love-interest bartender, and the killer was still thoroughly unknown to me (and likely off making quick work of the third victim). I shifted rightward on the couch, scrutinizing the bartender's forearm tattoo from a clearer angle.

"Do you really think someone with a rattlesnake tattoo can be trusted?"

"It's a very tasteful-looking rattlesnake, though," Joanna said. "As far as rattlesnake tattoos go."

I wrinkled my nose. I wasn't much feeling the chemistry between Nadia and the bartender; he was too wiry, too hipster-ish, too…

Un-Del-like.

And as if the thought had been a summons, the door behind me hissed open. I turned, and everything within me stilled at the sight of him. It was the first I'd seen him since the kiss.

Del is tall, broad, and strapping, ruddy in coloring, with a darker, coarse tumble of hair that spills down over his wide shoulders. He wears simple clothing that doesn't hide his physique: dark trousers that cut off at the knee, a thick, leathery strap that runs crosswise over his chest like a sash. It's a description that I suppose could sound like some human Fabio.

But there is no denying that he is unhuman. He has fur. His eyes are red-rimmed. He has brown-black claws and sharp fangs and a broad, flat nose and a pronounced brow. The overall effect is faintly leonine (though no tail).

And just like I had come to be able to read Joanna's mood

by her hue, so too had I come to be able to read his unhuman face. Right now he looked weary, sort of worn around the edges. I watched his eyes flick from me to the peachy-orange of the walls to the cauldron, which had paused mid-action. Nadia was leaning over the bar in a way that left little to the imagination. The bartender, bless him, had been caught with his eyes lowered toward her two assets on display.

"We're solving a murder," I explained. "Actually, two murders. Maybe three by now. The killer works quick."

"This is something she designed for you?" he asked, with a jerk of his chin toward the wall.

"Yes. And might I say she's doing a fantastic job, too." Joanna bloomed with a slight golden shimmer. I motioned to the couch beside me. "You… wouldn't want to join, would you?" The shimmering intensified.

Del voiced a few gruff words in Ziryahshun, and she faded out. "I can spare some time," he said to me.

"Well, only if you want to."

"I do want to," he said, his eyes intent on me. Whoa. Then in one quick, fluid motion he hopped over the back of the couch and settled just a scant few inches away from where I was sitting. Still, that distance felt wide as a gulf, what with the untouched subject of the kiss floating amorphously between us.

"So," I said, leaning on chatter to fill the space, "Nadia— that's the woman here—is a professional organizer. Oh, maybe you don't know what that is, since the bots take care of everything around here. Um, a professional organizer—"

"I can surmise what it is that they do."

"Right. Anyway, Nadia was at a job when she discovered a dead body—a very, very dead body. Flies, all swollen... it was disgusting. We've identified the victim as a young woman called Sue-Ann Henry."

"Mm."

"Sue-Ann wasn't the sharpest tool in the shed. Er, I mean, she wasn't too bright; all the people we've interviewed so far confirm that. But a very pretty woman. When she wasn't dead on a garage floor with flies all over her, that is. I mean, you should have *seen* how gross it was. The second victim is—"

"Corinne," he said, the tone of his voice implying wrangled patience, "I am sure it's a fascinating story." I turned and found him now leaning towards me, very close indeed.

"Y-yeah," I said, a bit dizzy.

"But the arrival of my sister—sisters—on the ship has placed a great deal of demand on my time." Lord, his eyes were mesmerizing this close up—darker flecks of garnet amongst the vermilion. "And," he continued, as my head swam, "I thought we might speak of yesterday... when..."

"Okay," I said shakily, and then I had a vision. I could scoot away from him, so that the electricity of his maleness wouldn't be zapping all coherent thoughts from my brain. And then we could progress through whatever awkward conversation he was aiming for.

Or, alternatively, I could just...

The latter option seemed much more fun—so I closed the distance between us and brushed my lips to his.

I could feel a shock go through him. But his surprise was

there and then gone; he was leaning into me, he was kissing me back, he was—oh! Pushing me down to the couch, and God, I loved the muscled length of him over me. I arched my back, pressing up to him; I could tell he was keeping some of his weight off me, fearful to crush me. He gave a pleased growl, one hand moving to the small of my back to clutch me to him, the other sliding down to my ass. And then I reached around him with both hands and tried to pull him downward.

He made a startled, guttural noise. "It's all right," I murmured. "We humans aren't so delicate as all that." He lowered himself slowly, cautiously, only coming all the way down when I made a little satisfied noise. I could have purred like a cat, he felt so good against me. I gave him a nip of a kiss on the nose, playing, and he gave me the same; I did it again, and he cupped both sides of my head in his hands and just... looked.

"Beautiful," he said at last, in that deep voice of his. "I haven't been able to look away since you first came here." A lock of hair had fallen over my face; he caught it between admiring fingers before softly brushing it away, then with the gentlest touch traced the side of my face—temple to ear, then down my jaw. I pressed into him, nuzzling his hand, and the small prick of his claws against my skin made me shiver.

Now it was my turn: I brought a wondering hand up to touch the short, velvety fur that covered his skin, then the unruly scraggle of his mane. I brushed a finger against the heavy sternness of his brow, the slant of his temple. His gaze stayed on me, rapt, through it all. Then, when my hand came to rest against his cheek, he closed his eyes. I had never seen him look so… free? Like some faint, unnoticed shadow had fled from his eyes.

I kissed him again, deeply, and the gravelly sound of pleasure he made in the back of his throat sent a warm rolling wave through me, a wave that said *yes*. Everything was right in the world, every worry and trouble suspended. If I could just stay here, in this moment, forever…

He sensed something was wrong before the thought had even fully formed in my mind. Pulling back, he searched my face.

"Are you—?"

"I don't know," I said, pulling myself out from underneath him. "I-I'm not sure if… Well…" I found myself standing now on shaky legs, twisting my hands against each other. Faint panic pressed on me from all directions, and I had to think, *I had to think*, but it wasn't going to happen with him right here, staring at me. "I'd better get back."

"Corinne—"

"Maybe later," I said, looking to the door, and he grabbed at the chance.

"Come see me tonight," he said. "If you'd like, that is. We can talk—just talk. Joanna can tell you when it's safe to come." His mouth twisted. "Jexrah… makes matters difficult…"

"She suspects something," I blurted as I clambered over the couch so I could get to the door. He needed to know—probably already did know—but I had to warn him, just in case.

Del bowed his head gravely. "Naturally. It would be unlike her not to suspect."

"Joanna messed with the security footage to cover up for my

dad leaving. Jexrah knows it's been doctored. If she finds out about my dad—"

He shook his head. "No. That, I can promise you, will not happen."

I gave him a sharp little nod, my mouth dry. His promise would have to be enough.

"Tonight?" he prompted. His expression was calm, but that shadow had returned to his face, and something in his eyes seemed to plead with me. At the sight, an inner part of me crumpled, turning black and miserable.

"I don't know," I said at last, and I didn't look at him as I said it. Then I fled back to my room, thoughts nipping at my heels like wolves.

Chapter Four

"I DON'T WANT TO TALK ABOUT IT," I SAID TO JOANNA AS I stormed back into my room. Lord knew what she'd seen and heard—probably everything. "But you'd better be able to hide all of it from Jexrah."

"Already done. We're now taking especial precautions to—"

"Don't care. Just as long as it works."

Midge had brought me over one of her tennis balls as a greeting. I took it from her numbly, even as I felt some unformed kernel of anger heat up in my chest. More than any other time I wished I had someone to spill my thoughts to, someone's shoulder to cry on—a *human*, not a dog. What I wouldn't give for a girls' night with Molly right now; how was I supposed to make any sense of this by myself?

Midge pressed against my legs. I'd been away too long; it was time to walk her. So back to the hothouse I went, striding quickly with Midge alongside me. I suppressed a shudder when the door slid open; the whole space felt sullied by my interaction with Jexrah that morning. While Midge trotted off to her usual patch to do her business, I selected a spot by the gazebo in need of weeding and went on the attack. And at last, my hands preoccupied with useful violence, I let my mind stray to what had happened.

I'd wanted to stay with him. In that moment, when the world around us had held its breath and time stood still, his embrace had felt too good, too right, and—I ripped a plant from the soil with unnecessary viciousness—I'd wanted to stay.

But it was a simple impossibility. There was my dad to think about, never mind my friends, my town, *Earth itself*. And on top of all those reasons, Del was a prince. Whoever he was supposed to end up with in the end, it wasn't me, a human girl from Wakpa. I didn't know the details, but surely there was a short list of eligible rumae ladies for Del to select a partner from, and there wasn't a chance my name was on it.

And how could I trust any of my feelings, with Del my only option? It was impossible for this attraction to be genuine. This was mere brain trickery—had to be.

The only logical choice was for this… *whatever* that was happening between us to end. I would tell him tonight. And also… my eyes wandered in the direction of the gazebo, where I'd stuffed my precious sulfur and saltpeter.

I whistled for Midge, and she emerged from the foliage a moment later, then did a full-body shake. A few stray burrs were stuck fast in her fur, and I frowned as I bent to pick them out. She had some secret pooping spot that I'd been meaning to check to make sure there weren't any canine hazards—but that could wait a day.

I pulled the last burr from her fur, then gave her a hug. "Time to go," I whispered in her ear, and her tail beat against the ground.

Yes, time to go—past time, really.

"Any seedlings yet?" Joanna asked when we rejoined her at the wall. Her voice had the false lightness of someone who doesn't want to cause a stir.

"No," I said. "Could be they just need more time to sprout, but I have a hunch that the moisture in the soil is the real issue. Too much opportunity for fungus and rot."

Her fractals swirled in thought. "It makes sense. But it's not practical to modify the watering cycle of the room to test that theory, unfortunately. Is that it, then? Are you wanting to put together a planter on the top deck?"

"Not yet. I'm going to replant, and this time I want to mix a layer of horticultural charcoal into the soil first. Just a last-ditch effort."

"I'm on it," she said.

Charcoal, sulfur, and saltpeter—it was the black powder trifecta. I'd gathered my ingredients; now I had to craft an escape out of them.

I brought Midge back to my room before heading to the hothouse yet again to spend the rest of the day "weeding." Work would get my head back on straight. Work would let me forget about Del, distract me from what I had to tell him tonight.

Joanna had supplied me with a big bag of horticultural charcoal, along with more seeds to replant. Back in the gazebo, I cupped the seeds in my hand and ate them; I couldn't risk any of the seeds escaping and sprouting accidentally. Next I spread a tarp over the ground and got to work, always listening for the sound of approaching footsteps—or the buzz of a drone.

Small particles, thoroughly mixed: that, Professor Thoner had always told us, was the key to good black powder. There was no conceivable reason for me to ask Joanna for a mortar and pestle, so I hunted for a worthy rock on the ground, then dumped out half my charcoal onto the thick tarp Joanna had fabricated for me a few days ago. Folding the tarp over to cover the charcoal, I began smashing it into powder with the rock. It was hard, tedious work, and soon my arm was trembling.

At last I had a small mound of black dust. I eyed it warily; would it be enough? The chemical ratio didn't call for much charcoal, but… I sighed and shook a few more of the charcoal bits onto the tarp, then wearily picked up the rock again.

When my little pile of charcoal powder had grown to a medium-sized handful, I tipped it into one of the leftover beakers from the soil test kit before washing the tarp down with some water from my metal thermos. The charcoal sluiced off the tarp's blue plastic in a dark gray dribble.

Now to do the same with the saltpeter and the sulfur. The sulfur, thankfully, was in soft yellow chunks that crumbled to fine dust in my hands—no rotten-egg smell, to my relief. The saltpeter could have passed for granulated sugar, and I flexed my hand back and forth before reaching for my rock again. By the time I was satisfied, my palm was red and smarting, and I could barely lift the rock.

But I had my three neat containers of black, white, and yellow powders. The soil test kit didn't include a scale, so I'd have to do my best to get the ratio right. I measured out a lot of this and a little of that onto the tarp in separate piles. Then took away some of the charcoal and added a smidgen more sulfur. Eyed my powders in silence for a while…

And added a tad more sulfur.

Then a few grains more.

A bit less saltpeter, perhaps?
Then again, maybe not.

What about the charcoal?
Add a pinch more. Or, say, half a pinch.
That's better… I hope.

Looked at the powders again for a few long minutes. Tightened my ponytail. Pulled on a fresh pair of nitrile gloves. Tried not to bite at my lip.

Said a silent prayer.

Then drizzled a bit of water from my thermos over all three powders and began to mix them together.

"Everything all right? Thought I heard banging," Joanna said when I finally made my way back down the white path to her.

"A tree root was pushing up part of the path. I had to pull out the stones, reroute the path, and put them back in again."

"Ah, makes sense," she said. "You hungry?"

I was listless through dinner, then listless through a chapter of *Emma*. It's tough to find distraction when you know there's a clayish mound of proto-gunpowder hidden just down the hall to dry.

I'd stashed the gunpowder in the pitcher trap of the dead, dried-out gohrrow plant, and buried my fabricated screw-top tumbler in the dirt just beside it. There my precious materials would be hidden from prying aliens, and the gunpowder would have the chance to dry out. Despite all my precautions, though, I still had no confidence the black powder would work. There were simply too many things that could go wrong: the ingredient ratio, the humidity in the room, the amount of water in the mix.

But... if it did work... that meant I had to start thinking more seriously about what I wanted to *do* with my gunpowder. This part of the plan had always been fuzzy. Blowing a hole in the side of the ship seemed possible, but getting back down to the ground—that was a different story. I couldn't just jump out and hope for the best—by my estimation the ship kept up a constant hover of at least seventy feet off the ground. Perhaps

I could tie the clothes from my ever-burgeoning wardrobe together into a clothes-ladder, then clamber down. With my dog strapped to my back.

Insanity—that's where this situation had landed me.

"Del's with Jexrah right now?" I asked Joanna. I was lying on the bed, Midge curled up into a snoring, fluffy ball beside me.

"Yes…" she said slowly. She sounded preoccupied with something.

I gave a tired nod, sinking back further into my pillow. My body ached, and I longed to follow Midge's example and go to sleep—but I had to talk to Del tonight, to tell him… My thoughts stuttered, and a queasiness washed over me.

Best not to think about it. I didn't want to plan out a speech—too dismissive, too juvenile. I'd just go to him when Joanna gave me the go-ahead, and—

"Corinne." Her voice was quiet, apologetic.

"What's up?" I said, trying to keep a calm lid over the dread that had just surged through me. This was it.

"Khindrae Jexrah—"

What?

"—apologizes for the late message, but she has prepared a special activity for you, herself, Khindrae Meervit, and the master."

"A special activity right *now?*"

"Yes," she said, her colors darkening. She had *don't shoot the messenger* written all over her.

"But… right now?" I repeated. "Really? What time is it even?"

"Quarter of ten." I blinked; across the room, the fabricator screen had snapped shut, its interior promptly aglow with orange light. "I'm making you an outfit," she said. "She expects you in ten minutes."

"Hang on now. This is ridic—" But I swallowed the thought, because, like it or not, I was scared of the khindrae. Best to go along with her inane power play—for that's what this was, clearly—so that I could ease her suspicions. "Fine," I said, sliding off the bed reluctantly. Midge pricked an ear, but didn't budge an inch otherwise. I gave her a jealous frown.

"Okay," said Joanna with obvious relief as the fabricator dinged.

I walked over to it and shrugged off my robe. The clothes inside were still steaming when I pulled them out for inspection. She'd made me a cloud-gray catsuit with a high turtleneck, wrist-length gloves in the same color, a pair of thin white socks, some sleek knee-high boots crafted from lightweight metal, and a shiny black helmet with a full face shield. The fabric of everything had that same odd slippy-but-strong feel as the clothes Del and I had worn to hunt the val—but all that had taken place in the sim room, and this was real life. A thought skittered through my brain: *Jexrah couldn't be trying to kill me, could she?*

"Clue me in, would you?" I said as I shimmied into the catsuit. It fit like a glove, and the fabric was breathable—none of that latex Catwoman nonsense.

"She wants to use the ship's escape pods for a night of stargazing. Not really their intended use, but the khindrae does as she pleases."

The world stood still around me. "Escape pods?" I breathed. And I could have shot myself after I said it, so obviously could I hear the yearning in my voice—but I'd concealed so much from Joanna by now, lied to her, manipulated her, that she didn't seem to notice. I was just the docile human, resigned to my abduction.

"No need to worry," she said. "You'll use a pre-programmed flight path."

"Right," I said, reaching for the high metal boots. Loose mesh loops let them splay open at the sides; as soon as I'd eased my feet in, the loops gave a slight hiss and cinched tight around my calves.

"Pre-programmed, huh?" I asked, taking a few tentative steps. Walking was clunky—but I supposed the boots were for flying, not walking, after all. "And who programmed it—Miss Alien Princess?"

"I've checked the flight path. You'll be perfectly safe."

"Mm-hm," I said, pulling on the gloves. "Sure." With the helmet under my arm, I walked over to the mirror to take a look at the full ensemble. I looked... cool. A bit like I was dressed up for a Daft Punk concert.

"Minigolf seems like it would be much easier," I said wistfully to my reflection.

"Perhaps you could suggest it to the khindrae for your next outing." She gave a little blue pulse. "Er, but don't really do that. Probably best for you to just lay low."

"Bowling, then? Or maybe a relaxing day of bird-watching?"

"Time to get going!" she said in a chipper voice.

"Of course. Wouldn't want to keep the khindrae waiting, would we?"

Arlene Wint liked to think her three decades dedicated to keeping Wakpa's finest drinking establishment up and running should qualify her for some sort of honorary degree. A PhD in social psychology seemed about right, perhaps with a focus on the interplay between alcohol consumption and sexual relationships. She could have dashed off dissertations in her sleep.

Take the brunette girl at the far end of the bar, for example, currently being plied with drinks by the flannel-clad young man beside her. It wasn't going to work out; Arlene could tell that straightaway by how the girl kept sneaking glances at her phone. Her hopeful Romeo should have been able to see that, if he hadn't had a couple shots himself.

Then there was the young couple over by the door. Pretty blond girl, cute as a button—Francine and Milo Buie's daughter, if Arlene had her family trees right. Her name started with an *M*, didn't it—Mary? No, that wasn't it. Molly—that sounded right. And her husband was… Kurt something. Anyway, the two of them had seemingly adopted shit-talking each other as a mutual pastime, but one glance was all you needed to see the love between them. He'd ordered an IPA, and she'd gone for a milkshake. Maybe pregnant? Huh. Well, the way she was sipping out of that straw and looking at Kurt said he'd be a happy man tonight, at any rate.

Now what about the young man in the corner booth with his buddies? That same Joe Gagnon she'd witnessed get his heart broken by that blond beauty—Walt Kaminski's daughter. Poor guy; you could tell from the set of his face that he was taking it hard. Sure, he was out with friends, but he might as well have been drinking alone. On his third beer already, not really looking at anything in particular—your classic case of the down-in-the-dumps. Maybe mixed with a bit of *she-was-the-one*-itis. And hadn't he been in here a couple other times this week, looking the same way?

Oh well, he'd just have to do his pining, then move on; word was Corinne Kaminski was down in Texas right now, having gotten the hell out of Dodge after the breakup. And Lord knew Arlene could have given Joe a bucketload of advice, but—she shook her head—these kids never wanted to listen.

Time would teach him; she was sure of it.

Chapter Five

I DODDERED INTO THE ESCAPE-POD ROOM THOROUGHLY pleased that I was three and a half minutes late.

This was one of the slew of the rooms that had been forbidden to me, and I looked around curiously. The room had none of the luxury feel of the rest of the ship; it was little more than a plastic and metal cube. An enormous inset screen embedded in one wall glowed with a collection of graphs and charts. A few bucket seats were arranged in a circle in the middle of the room; they had a sort of oversized toddler's car seat design to them. Nothing looked like an escape pod.

Del and Jexrah stood together beside the seats, both suited up similarly to me, and—not Meervit. Del looked at me, his eyes dark and inscrutable, and I did my best to keep my own face a mask. In my chest, though, my traitorous heart leapt at the sight of him.

I turned my gaze toward Jexrah. "I thought M—*Khindrae* Meervit was going to be joining us." *Docility and deference— that's me! No matter about the gunpowder in the hothouse!*

"She is," said Jexrah sweetly. "My sister decided last minute that she'll be coming along for the ride in your pod."

"But…" I looked around again for Meervit's drone.

"No, dear, she'll be *in* your pod. Acting *as* the pod." Her eyes glittered as she watched me digest this. Oh, how I hated her—let me count the ways.

"How—how lovely," I said with a sinking feeling. What the hell, Joanna? That didn't sound like a pre-programmed flight path at all. That sounded like a choice opportunity for the alien princess to nose-dive me into the ground from the comfort of her home back on Tenctah.

"She had expressed interest in getting to know you, so I thought this would be a perfect opportunity."

"What fun," I said brightly. The khindrae wanted to get to know me? Maybe in the same way a cat toys with a mouse before killing it. "And where are the pods?"

Jexrah feigned a start of surprise. "Why, right here!" She gestured to the bucket seats.

"Is that right?" I said, giving the seat nearest me a nudge with the toe of my metal boot. Too late I wondered if I had just committed a capital offense by kicking Khindrae Meervit, but neither Jexrah nor Del reacted in horror, though the seat uttered a tinny *beep-boop* noise and the graphs on the screen in the wall jolted excitedly. Okay, so this really was a high-tech operation. From the corner of my eye, I spied Jexrah watching on with clear amusement. Silly, silly human, to not even know what a proper escape pod looked like.

"Helmets on," Del said gruffly. It was obvious enough that

he wasn't any happier about this late-night escapade than I was, but there was nothing to be done about it. Jexrah had her suspicions, and it was up to us to assuage them.

And maybe it would be fun. There was always that possibility, right?

The helmet fit snugly over my head, and the darkened glass of the face shield tinted the world a smoky hue.

"It fits well?" Del asked me, his voice muted through the helmet. I waggled my head back and forth, testing the fit. It was quite heavy and pressed a little uncomfortably on my neck, but it didn't feel like it was about to fly off, and that was the main thing, I supposed.

I nodded, bobblehead-like. "Feels good."

"Then sit down," he said, and he knelt to do just that. I followed his lead and picked the seat right next to his, and Jexrah took the one on his other side, so that moments later we were all seated in a semi-circle. Like the rest of the furniture on the ship, the seat was overlarge, but the cushioning was comfortable enough. The reclined angle of the seat reminded me of a movie theater. Watching a movie—that would have been another recreational activity less perilous than letting Del's sister power an escape pod with me in it. Oh well.

I turned to Del to ask him what came next, but there was a sudden, alarming slithering along my spine, under the fabric of the chair. I yelped as long metal straps sprang forth from both sides of the seat. They wriggled in the air above me like tentacles, before weaving themselves lickety-split into a criss-cross pattern to bind me to the seat, snug as a swaddled baby.

"Well," I said, drawing a short, shuddering breath. "That's definitely the most horrifying thing that's happened to me all day."

"You'll feel—" Del started, but I didn't hear anything else; another metal tendril was snaking along the nape of my neck to hook into my helmet and jerk my head back so it lay flush against the seat. And now something down below, too, latched onto my boots, anchoring them in place.

I considered screaming, but decided against it. It would give Jexrah too much satisfaction.

"Hello there," said an accented female voice in my ear.

I screamed. From two seats down, I felt Jexrah smile.

"Don't be alarmed," said the disembodied voice—always exactly the wrong thing to say. "This next part might surprise you."

And then a thin, liquid iridescence flowed into my vision. Just a scant foot above my head, it curled up and over the seat like a sentient wave, bathing me in an unearthly, shifting light, before stretching down toward my legs. Within seconds the whole seat was encapsulated, like someone had blown a giant soap bubble and trapped me within.

"There we are," said Meervit softly from the speaker in my helmet. "Now give me a second." I heard a soft fizz; sparks shimmered within the goop, and the bubble twitched in response, here caving inward, there billowing outward. And I gasped as the bubble became sleek, its form refined… She was making it aerodynamic—the nose of the bubble needle-sharp, the sides bent into curves and whorls.

The seat beneath me thrummed as mechanisms powered on. There was a series of beeps, and a robotic voice began listing something in Ziryahshun.

"Don't forget to breathe," Meervit said. "We're going in a second."

"What—?"

But there was no time for questions. From beneath the seat came the low, scraping groan of gears, and then an insistent wind rushed into the room and the floor fell away, tipping my seat and the bubble outward into open air.

Chapter Six

THE POD PLUNGED DOWNWARD, AND ALL I COULD THINK WAS how nicely pointed the treetops were—perfect for popping bubbles.

Then a puff of wind caught the pod, and with a jerk we went airborne. The pod spun dizzyingly, the world a churning mash of ground, sky, and spaceship—and stabilized at last. Above my head the bubble gleamed like polished glass, and above that…

"Your planet is very beautiful," Meervit said quietly in my ear. "And I have seen quite a lot of them."

There was the sky, in all its nighttime splendor. It was one of those rare, clear winter nights; the moon, almost full, hung high like a silver coin, and stars pierced the black of the sky like diamond dust.

And I was finally outside the ship, for the first time in… I'd lost track of the days. Buoyed by the light breeze and a prayer, the pod slid through the air like a fish through calm water. The seat's hold on my helmet and feet released, and the straps across my body loosened with a soft hiss.

"You can sit up now," Meervit said. "We're aloft."

The ship was the first thing I saw when I pushed myself up to take a look around. I knew the *Huivnarrut* well enough on the inside, but its exterior had remained a mystery to me. All I'd seen of the ship before I'd come aboard had been that glittering black hole in the sky, drawing me upwards.

It wasn't what you'd think of at all if someone said the words *alien spaceship*. No flying saucer here—the ship may have been crafted from metal, but it looked like a thing organic. Its main body was a silvery green, the surface sort of dimpled, like a walnut. Lissome offshoots of metal wreathed the body of the ship like cupped fingers, and these radiated a reddish light that shimmered with heat. The whole ship floated thirty feet or so above the treetops, and though it wasn't moving, it had a quivering energy about it. I was reminded of a hummingbird paused mid-flight.

"Wow," I breathed, as my mind went taut. All it took was one look at the *Huivnarrut* and you could see its potential—there one second and gone the next, zipping away into space in an instant.

Which made it all the more important to use this time to work out how I could steal an escape pod.

First things first, though, I had to know what I was stealing. "Can I touch it?" I asked, motioning at the bubble.

"Go ahead."

I brushed my fingers against the bubble wonderingly. It was smooth as silk and rippled gently under my touch. The material was vaguely oily, though my fingers came away clean.

"It's a material based off the DNA of a very singular creature called the *ilta roh*," Meervit said, anticipating my question. "The ilta roh are tiny organisms, near microscopic, that cluster in schools in the upper reaches of Tenctah's atmosphere. The conditions are punishing, if you can imagine—scarcely any oxygen, bitterly cold. But the unique qualities of the creatures' outer membranes allow them to survive. And to thrive, even.

"So our scientists used the base DNA of the ilta roh to make sturdier, safer escape pods than anything we'd produced previously. I know it doesn't look like much, but this pod can withstand lengthy periods of deep space travel before decomposing. Evolution, as it turns out, can craft a better technology than anything we can come up with ourselves."

Against my better judgment, I found myself relaxing as she spoke. Call it some combination of her cool, accented voice, or the smooth way we were gliding through the air, or the freedom of the open sky above. Probably the two sisters were in cahoots and I was under the sway of a good cop, bad cop routine. Regardless, I was almost liking this sister, and that feeling only grew at the next thing she said.

"I wanted to apologize for scaring your animal."

I blinked, startled. "Th-that's all right. I'd heard it had something to do with, er, snap travel." Like I knew what that was.

"It's quite cute—your animal."

I grinned under the helmet. "Thanks. She's a dog. Her name's Midge."

"She must be a real comfort for you in this situation."

"Oh, definitely," I said, my eyes still on the strange metal mass of the *Huivnarrut*. Where in there was my room, or the hothouse? "I… don't know what I'd do without her. Oh, I just realized—where's your sister's ship?"

"Ah," she said, and the pod nosed a new course through the air. "I'll show you." For a second, before we floated away, a blotch of wrongness near the bottom of the ship caught my eye, dark and tumorous. That had to be the room in Del's quarters—that cold, desolate room that formed the basis for my escape plan. What in the world had torn the ship apart like that?

"Here it is," said Meervit, drawing me back to the present. Jexrah's ship, sleeker and smaller than the *Huivnarrut*, had just come into view, hovering alongside the larger ship. It was about a fourth the size of the *Huivnarrut*, the exterior a sharp yellow with accented black. I snorted.

"What is it?" asked Meervit.

"I was just thinking it looks like a wasp." And that matched the alien princess perfectly, didn't it?

"Its name would translate to something like… *Bolt*." She began gently winging us away.

"It's a race car? Race… ship?"

Without warning, the *Huivnarrut* blinked into nothingness, only its background of shadowed mountains and star-smattered sky remaining. Its disappearing act was echoed by Jexrah's ship vanishing a moment later.

"What—?"

"Oh, they're both still there," Meervit said, nonchalant. "A cloaking security measure, now that we're a distance away. Anyway, her ship *is* quite fast. My sister can be somewhat of a daredevil. We all are. It runs in the family."

No need to tell me. I'd seen the way Del had tackled those val. "So," I said, settling back down into the seat. The supposed point of this outing was to stargaze, after all. "What made you decide to come along for the ride with Khindrae Jexrah? Just a fun road trip? Er…" English really had a lot of growing to do when it came to communicating with a spacefaring race.

"You could say that," she said, rather delicately. "It had been too long since I'd seen him. I missed him."

"Hm. I thought…" I frowned. Now it was time for me to speak delicately; I didn't want to offend her. "Someone had told me that you… um… have many drones stationed in different locations. I would have thought…" I trailed into silence, not sure how to phrase, *I would have thought you'd have a drone on board the* Huivnarrut, *so you could see your own brother whenever you like.* Or maybe rumae siblings didn't work like that—maybe the ties between them were weaker than that of humans.

And then, with a click of realization, my déjà vu at the sight of Meervit the day before finally resolved itself—because I actually *had* seen her before, or some carbon copy of her, when I'd first gone room to room searching the ship. Hadn't there been a drone stashed in a closet just the same as her, with its mosquito-ish body and large, sleepy orb eye?

It had to be her.

"The drone on my brother's ship is unfortunately broken,"

Meervit said simply. "So when my sister told me she was going to pay him a visit, I decided to come along."

"Right," I said, as my brain picked apart those syllables. *Unfortunately broken.* There were a quite a lot of things on board that were unfortunately broken, weren't there? And perhaps the drone had been damaged in whatever catastrophe had caused the other destruction to the ship—but, then again, there was that mirror, scratched beyond repair in Del's room… Scratched purposely so.

The quiet of the night enveloped the pod. The sky spread above us like a quilt of black and silver. I squinted, trying to remember my constellations. I don't know any more than most people; I can spot the Big Dipper and maybe Orion's Belt. The rumae must have their own stories about the stars—legends, mythologies. I'd never discussed religion with Del; was there something his people believed in? I'd have to ask…

But instead I took a steadying breath and said softly, "There must be quite a lot that can go wrong with your drones."

A too long pause. "Very true."

"Has anyone ever, er… tampered with them? You're a princess—well, a khindrae, I mean. I'm sure there could be a… sort of situation… where someone might not want you to drop in."

"It… has happened before."

"Sounds frustrating."

"Yes. And… worrisome."

"I can imagine."

A pregnant silence gripped the pod again, and I was on the verge of telling Meervit to just spill the beans already when a blur severed the night sky: Jexrah, rocketing through the air at breakneck speed. Through the helmet I could see a maniacal grin on her face.

"My sister," Meervit said, with a sort of weary acceptance. "Like I said, she's a bold sort."

"You the older sister?"

"I am, if only by a few minutes."

"Still counts."

"That," she said, turning the pod in Jexrah's direction, "is what I always tell her, yet somehow I never seem to be afforded my due sororal deference." I laughed as we went to join the others, feeling like both quite a lot and nothing at all had been said between us.

Del was hovering in his pod, stretched out long to watch the stars. His eyes flicked toward me when I drew near, but for just a moment only—there could be no hint of what had happened between us. Jexrah, meanwhile, was zipping around like she was practicing to be a fighter pilot. She'd reclined her seat so that it lay fully horizontal, with her stomach facing the ground like Superman. Her pod's bubble had lengthened and stretched too, each curve long and sharp as a knife. She cut through the air with a whiffing noise.

"Enjoying the night?" she called as she zoomed by, her words distorted by the speed and the helmet.

"Not as much as you," I answered. Doubtful she heard me; she was already half a football field away.

Meervit winged us nearer to Del. The walls of our two pods trembled and shimmered with oily rainbows as they drew close, like they could sense each other's presence through the air. And then, just as collision seemed imminent, the bubbles stretched out with wire-thin tendrils toward each other to bridge the gap and merged. After a moment of reconfiguration Del and I were side by side, floating midair, the glossy membrane separating us beating a hasty retreat.

"Hi," I said.

He gave a nod and a princely "hello," but that was it. And I supposed that made sense, since his sister was in the walls serving as de facto chaperone, but it still stung.

I settled back to look at the stars, only to start with a jerk when Jexrah zipped by again. Quick as anything Del reached out, a sort of reflexive movement, and his palm brushed mine. I drew a minuscule, hissing breath between my teeth—nothing that anyone should properly notice—but he did. My hand was still raw from grinding my chemicals into powder.

"Nothing," I breathed at the look of confusion he shot me through the helmet. God, you couldn't let the two of us together for a minute. Was Meervit sharp enough to make anything of those bumbling few seconds? I nestled back into my seat and closed my eyes, trying to pretend I was anywhere but here.

A few minutes passed. Five. Maybe ten. Was it more suspicious for us not to talk at all? Perhaps it made more sense for the alien prince and his abductee to keep up some bored small talk. I was just opening my mouth to say something, *anything*, when Jexrah careened toward us again and came to a stop this time. She looked exhilarated, almost giddy. If it hadn't been for her flying outfit, I was sure her every hair would be standing on end.

"The air here is amazing!"

With effort, I repressed the urge to say, *you're welcome*.

"You should take a turn around," she continued with a look to her brother.

He shifted in his seat. "Another time."

"Surely you—" she started, but with another look from him she caught herself. She might be a spy sent by their mother, but the chain of command still counted for something—he remained the heir apparent, outweighing her mere royalty.

And royals like Jexrah, predictably, didn't like being reminded of that. Her gaze swung around to me. "Then how about it?"

"H-how about what?"

"A ride around."

My stomach did a little flip. I've never been one for fair rides or roller coasters. "I could never—"

"Oh, but you must!" she insisted with an encouraging smile that I wished I could smack off her face. *You must—because I am a princess, and you are a nobody.* And of course Del couldn't intervene, because I was supposed to be a nobody to him, too. "My sister will be in control, of course."

"I will be," said Meervit in my ear. "I can take it slow for you."

"Well, all right," I said, blasting Jexrah with my best customer-service smile. *Fuck you, bitch. Fuck you to whatever the rumae equivalent of hell is.*

Then began a quick reconfiguration of my pod to make it race-worthy: my bubble separated from Del's once more; my seat reclined all the way back; the seatbelt-tentacles tightened;

the membrane's shape grew yet more honed, sort of Indy car-like. All that taken care of, the whole pod then flipped upside down, so that the stars were at my back, the sheer drop to the ground never more apparent.

"Better to look forward than down," Meervit murmured.

"Got it," I said weakly.

And we were off, shooting into the darkness. The radiating light of the ship became mere memory in just a few seconds; the jet-black of the night closed in, and I felt, more than saw, the pod slicing through the air. We were climbing; I could tell by the pop of my ears. Suddenly, disgruntled flapping, an angry cry, and a patch of darkness to the right bolted away—

The pod bucked a little. "What—?"

"An owl!" I cried, laughing from shock. "Or a hawk. Probably that, we're so high. Don't you dare dive!" She was maintaining our upward trajectory; God only knew what altitude we were at by now.

"I won't." Higher and higher and higher we climbed, the air parting for us sibilantly. A fine mist clung to the pod's membrane as we dashed through a low-hanging cloud, the moisture whisked away in thin rivulets a moment later when we emerged from the other side. "The sensors were indicating that tonight might be a good night… Well, I just wanted to see—ah!"

We slowed, the pod flipping around, so I could see the stars again…

A green luminescence split the sky in long, shimmering streamers. And as we drifted ever higher, a soft electrical whistling joined the swooshing of the nighttime wind, like a pod of spirit dolphins were dancing all around us. My mouth fell open.

"Incredible," said Meervit, in a bare whisper. There wasn't a soul around us, but it still felt like the sort of thing you should whisper for, like we'd entered a temple. "Have you ever seen—?"

"No, I haven't—not really." I'd seen a greeny hint of the northern lights once or twice, glowing far off in the distance, but never so strong, never like this. "Oh my God. It's so beautiful." Because that was really all you could say.

Together, we watched the aurora dance through the sky, as the not-dolphins serenaded us with their gentle susurration. I'd never considered that the northern lights might make noise, but now that I'd heard the otherworldly sound, I couldn't imagine the lights any other way. Once every so often a foggy red or white would stain the green, before sliding away into the night. If you looked at the aurora the right way, maybe let your eyes glaze over a bit, you could almost imagine it was a dragon's great, curving tail, lashing slowly across the sky as it flew overhead.

"Perhaps we should get going," Meervit said after a while.

"Yeah…" And then we didn't get going, because turning your back on the northern lights to head home felt like some sort of sacrilege. Time passed. The world shrunk and expanded, me a little dot of life under all that infinite green and black.

"I'm worried about my brother," Meervit said. It was such a quick, unexpected statement that I almost thought I'd imagined it. But I could understand why she'd felt free to say it, finally. With nature's majesty before us, what value did mortal secrets hold?

"I can tell that you are."

"I'm sure. We are all worried about him, in our different ways and for different reasons. My mother, my siblings. Even some of those in the… I think you might call it the court."

"And Joanna," I added. "His ship steward."

"Yes, naturally. Exactly. So I was wondering, since you've been with him this past while, that perhaps you might have some insight…"

"I don't know," I said, shaking my head. The nose of the pod dipped a little, and I could imagine the unseen khindrae wilting. And I wanted to help her, truly, but how could I, when all I had was a jumble of suppositions and odd moments? The way he could flee suddenly from a conversation. All that time he spent shut away downstairs, working on… something. The mirror. The shadows that clouded his eyes. The changed name of the ship itself. How could you fit those disparate, broken pieces together to form something solid?

"I need to know what happened to the ship," I said. "Do you know?"

"Yes. Most of it."

"Just give me a little more to go on."

The not-dolphins crooned gently to each other. The wind calmed to a bare breeze. The aurora swirled above us like green fire.

And at long last, the khindrae said, "All right."

Chapter Seven

"You know a little about us, I'm assuming?" she asked me.

"A little. He's shown me Tenctah, from space, and Ailopt. We've talked about… this and that." This and that and little in between.

"Good," she said. "And what of the governing structure of Ailopt?"

"He's the heir apparent—the vra-khinahar. And…" I squinted, trying to think back to how Del had described it. "There are some officials below him…" A ruling body, I think he'd called them. I'd vaguely envisioned something like England's system—with the crucial difference, of course, being that Del would serve as much more than a mere monarchical figurehead.

"Yes. For us rumae, it's a system that has borne the test of time." Something unspoken lingered at the end of that sentence. "As I understand it," she continued, "on Earth monarchies are widely considered now to be an outdated mode of governance. The hereditary dynasties of your world's history might be viewed as little more than a… a dominating mafia.

Hence the many power struggles, competing claims to the throne, et cetera."

I frowned, trying to sort through all the poli-sci talk. "You make it sound like all that's in the past. We don't exactly have everything figured out on Earth."

"Not my intention at all," she said. "Nor do my people have it all 'figured out,' I should add. But the system that seems to work best for us rumae is monarchical in structure. Differences in rumae and human genetic predispositions, I imagine."

"So…?"

"So what does that have to do with anything?" I tried to nod, but the apparatus hooking my helmet to the seat kept my head still. "Well," she continued, "in recent times my family has faced a growing—hm, I shouldn't say it's necessarily a growing *problem*. More of a concern. My people's success has bred new challenges. We moved past old-world manufacturing, discovered snap travel, took to the stars… and in the midst of all that innovation, several Ailoptian companies grew exceedingly wealthy and powerful."

It wasn't at all the direction I'd thought she was headed. "What do these companies do?"

"The question should be, what *don't* they do? If a private company manufactures weapons for your warforce, supplies power to your people, positions itself to be on the cutting edge of new technology—at what point do they rule and you follow? And true to form, these few companies structured themselves in a similar way to our royalty, with a ruling head, an heir apparent, and all the rest."

Now it began to come together, a little. "There's a competing royal family."

"Yes. Two of them, to be exact, and one a semi-distant third. So they involve themselves in any number of aspects of society, and we maintain a careful dance around each other. It's a silent sort of war, and mutual cooperation, in most cases, has remained the winning strategy. But things do happen…" She slid into silence for a moment, as the aurora beat a twisting path through the sky. "This information… you cannot share it with anyone. It's a matter we've kept very quiet."

"If I go to Tenctah, I don't expect I'll lead a normal life. Probably there won't be anyone to really share it with."

"Likely not," she said to be polite, when we both knew she meant, *definitely not.* "All right. My brother… he's a daredevil like the rest of us."

"I've noticed," I said dryly. "He took me val hunting, you know. In the ship's sim room."

"He—" I could tell by her voice that I'd surprised her. "Really?"

"Yeah." In a few sentences I took her through the whole bloody experience, excising the bit where we'd made out, of course.

"It seems you're quite tough," she said, somewhat wonderingly.

"I do my best. What were you saying, though, about your brother?"

"Right. He'd left the planet for a visit to Dru Gham—a mining planet we exhausted of resources a century or so ago. It's a desolate little planet, no life to speak of, expensive to get to by snap travel. Awful storms, as well."

"Sounds nice."

"No, not at all… Oh, I see what you mean. Hm." These rumae really needed a lesson in sarcasm. "In any case, we mined the planet until it was thoroughly depleted of resources, and the process left Dru Gham riddled with fissures and caves. We wouldn't strip a planet with life in such a way, but like I said—lifeless, and no one else seemed to have laid claim to it. And the geologic configuration of the Dru Gham rifts, it turns out, are perfectly suited to those who enjoy pod-racing—craft much like this." She punctuated her sentence by bobbing the nose of our escape pod gently.

"So Dru Gham has gained some notoriety with thrill seekers— but only those with the proper funds and ship capabilities can manage the journey to that area of space. My brother paid Dru Gham a visit, imagining the planet would be deserted. He was wrong.

"The eldest son of our most powerful competitor was already there, accompanied by his bodyguard and a few friends. My brother was attended by his one bodyguard alone. Given the mismatch in numbers, the best option would have been to turn around and go, quietly. But he wasn't afforded an opportunity to leave—too quickly they detected my brother's ship, and leaving would have sent the wrong political message. The other ship flashed a signal to him… and words were exchanged. They arranged a competition, of course."

"Men."

"*Heirs*," she corrected me. "I would have done the same thing, in his position. Any of us would have. The number of times I've told him—" She bit off her sentence in frustration.

"So now there was to be a race between the two of them, which they held, and naturally things got out of hand. There was an accident. Ahmpo's pod was wrecked—Ahmpo is the heir—and my brother's pod didn't fare much better. Ahmpo accused my brother of pulling a maneuver that had caused them to crash, and he demanded a rematch. My brother made some retort— he wouldn't again race someone so lacking in experience, some such like that. More words, tensions rose higher and higher, and a duel became the obvious option."

"A *duel*?" I tried to picture the laser-gun equivalent of a Wild West gunfight and shuddered. It sounded like an efficient way to make a nice heap of body parts.

"Not between the two of them, but using their personal guards as representatives. It's a tradition used in honor disputes for those above a certain social status. Not common… but not especially uncommon."

She sank into silence. The northern lights were fading out by now, dark night subsuming the mystical green. I could sense the next part of the story coming, hazy and malformed still, but soaked through with something bitter… something awful.

"He was close with his guard," she said finally. "Closer than it was wise, perhaps, to be. But… the guard had been assigned to my brother's security detail just a year into his royal service, when Delklor was just a child. So they spent many years together in close capacity, and… with their difference in age… Our father died when all of us were quite young, you know."

I thought that over for a moment. "De—Vra-khinahar Delklor saw his guard as a father figure."

"Yes. And... just a little while before all this occurred, the guard had respectfully requested a transfer. He saw matters for what they were—him getting older, physically, and my brother poised to come into his own as a leader, which would only increase Delklor's need for infallible security. So he requested a transfer, and my brother deferred granting it, for... sentimental reasons." She said these last two words like she was revealing a shameful secret. Leaders of nations with more than two and a half billion people weren't supposed to let feelings make decisions for them.

"The guard died in the duel," I said, not quite asking. A deep ache was spreading through my chest.

"He did. In a quite... painful manner. And afterward, when my brother was departing Dru Gham, Ahmpo's ship fired on him—not so as to destroy the ship completely, but as a taunt. A fluke malfunction on the part of their ship steward, they claimed, with half apologies." Meervit's tone said exactly what she thought about that.

"But isn't that illegal?"

"Legalities in that corner of space are murky. Dru Gham belongs to no one; we mined it, yes, but that doesn't necessarily mean our laws apply there. But putting the law aside, the only reasonable option was to let things lie. The power of Ahmpo's family cannot be overstated. A onetime squabble between heirs—that's all we can allow this to be, for now."

"And then Del came here," I said to finish the story.

"Yes, once the ship's snap-travel system was up and running again, he limped over to Earth. It was a convenient planet for him to undergo all the necessary repairs. And… now he is still here. We waited for his return, understanding it might take some time—there were the repairs to be completed, and his guard to grieve. But time stretched on. And he seemed different in our conversations—when he did speak with any of us, which wasn't often. A bit like he was… playacting as himself."

In my mind, Del's presence on Earth had always begun the day my father found his way onto the ship. That didn't make sense, of course, but somehow I'd never wondered when he'd arrived on Earth. Yet from what she was saying… "How long has your brother been here?"

"Nearly three of your Earth months."

"Three months!"

"You can see why we would be concerned. Please, Corinne—is there anything you can tell me? Something he's said or done."

There was so much he'd said and done, all of it secret, none of it relevant. I regretted telling her about us val-hunting together—stupid good cop, bad cop routine. More and more with these sisters I felt like a bug struggling in a spiderweb; each piece of information, whether given or taken, only drew me in deeper toward disaster. Even so, I felt bad for Meervit, and my heart ached for Del and his secret grief. "I don't know," I said honestly. "He hasn't mentioned any of this."

The pod gave a little shudder, and the khindrae stayed quiet. I wracked my brains, trying to think. "I really don't know. Maybe he just needs more time. Maybe—"

But now the pod trembled again as a rush of wind from over

the mountains gusted into us. "Khindrae Meervit?" I asked. "Hello?"

Her voice, when it came, was a jumble of static. "Corin— Think it's the sto— Try to—"

Then she cut out entirely, and the speaker in my helmet chimed and jabbered a few words in Ziryahshun—likely something along the lines of, *make your peace with God*, or maybe, *good luck, champ*. We were at a stationary hover still… weren't we? It was hard to be sure of anything in the dark, in the air, through my rising panic. But now I could feel the pod listing to the side a little… then sinking slowly, less slowly, really starting to go down now. Whenever I moved in the seat the pod jerked in response, but not in any sort of way I could understand how to control. It was like I'd just added a wild extra limb to my body, and that limb was hell-bent on self-destruction.

So I flailed against my seat restraints, trying to work it out and loosing some words that this pocket of airspace had likely never heard, nor ever would again. If I pushed into the seat with my legs that seemed to do something—same too with my elbows… I pushed my right arm into the seat and yelped when the pod jolted forward—and forward right now meant rushing down toward the stony embrace of the mountains.

Against every screaming instinct I relaxed my body, letting my arms and legs loosen, and the pod slowed. I was on the verge of understanding this machine, could feel one last part of the equation hovering just beyond my reach. I shut my eyes, tried to envision myself in the seat from above, what that might look like, the different pressure points of the seat... Then it hit me.

I was too short. It was the Goldilocks and the Three Bears problem—I was a human, in something constructed for a rumae, and that meant whatever touchpads I was hitting weren't lining up correctly with my body. I'd always been quite satisfied with my five feet five inches, but now I found myself wishing I'd drunk more milk as a kid.

No help for it—I'd have to stretch. I squirmed beneath the seat restraints, a contortionist struggling to escape a strait-jacket, trying to push my arms over my head. Muscles screamed, joints popped, and the seat sensors took my wriggling as a sign that, in addition to continuing our travel ever downward, it was time to swing the nose of the pod back and forth in a pendulous half-circle.

One last scream—*over to the right*—a violent push—*and over to the left*... My arm came free! I clawed the fabric of the seat above my helmet, and the pod's nose shot up to the sky, like a wolf raising its head to howl at the moon. But upward was good, upward was life, and as I withdrew some of the pressure on the seat the pod righted itself, until I was near level with the horizon. And now that I'd placed the missing puzzle piece, the controls were coming together to make some odd sense. *Lean this way and we head right, apply pressure there and the nose lowers. Dig your heels in like that and we go...*

Fast! I skimmed above the treetops, the world a dark blur, and a giddy wave of adrenaline coursed through me, tempered a moment later by that old, familiar fear. But there were no deer up here, just myself and the night sky and a bird or two—an unforeseen moment of freedom, the first time I'd really been alone in weeks.

I slowed to a midair halt, thoughts racing in all directions. I could head home—screw the gunpowder drying right now in the hothouse. The plan was too far-fetched to work; better to cut my losses and run.

But were those losses too great to withstand? There was Midge, for one. I could see her now, nestled into the pillows on the bed, ready to get up and greet me the second I came back. But I'd be gone forever, and she'd wait for me, one ear pricked for her human that wasn't to return. My heart broke just thinking about it.

And Del—I had to admit that the idea of fleeing into the night without seeing him one last time felt... more than wrong. Almost sickening. After everything Meervit had told me, not to mention the way I'd sprung away from him that last time we'd kissed... and he'd wanted to talk with me, had asked me to visit him with that pleading look in his eyes.

I nudged the pod forward, just to test my newfound freedom, and loosed a frustrated cry when some instinct stayed me from accelerating. What was the matter with me? "Go on," I whispered as the wind picked up, its sound an eerie keening. "Go on. Go on. Go on." My whispers turned ragged, until I was choking back tears, and something within me was fragmenting, leaving me all raw, jagged edges. I cried out again, my voice twining with the wind's howl...

A force barreled into me, knocking the pod end over end.

An arm snaked around my seat—Del's arm, I knew—and tugged me close, our two pod bubbles coalescing, and now he was shouting at me in Ziryahshun, his voice raised not from anger but fright. I could see his panicked face through his helmet, eyes raking over me to check that I was all right, and there could be no denying it now—I longed to be back in that room alone with him, in his arms. "I'm sorry," I gasped, "I'm so sorry"—but who was the apology even meant for? For my dad, because I hadn't been able to pull the trigger? For Del, because I'd thought about it?

Or for me, because in that moment I knew there was to be no fixing this?

Chapter Eight

THE SAME GEOMAGNETIC STORM THAT HAD CREATED SUCH beautiful aurora had also knocked out Meervit's connection with the pod, Del explained to me while we headed back to the ship. Like Icarus, we'd simply drifted a bit too high; any lower and there would never have been any issue. Jexrah and Del had realized straightaway that their sister had lost the connection; he'd been racing to come get me when he'd heard me shouting and assumed the pod was about to nose-dive.

Back on the ship, Jexrah was waiting for us, her helmet tucked under her arm. "Have fun?" she asked me brightly after Del docked our pods and I clambered from the seat. I gave her a look that I'm sure was more grimace than smile.

"*So* much fun," I said, clinging to my composure by a hair. For the umpteenth time, I wondered how in league Jexrah was with her sister. The northern lights had been dying down—wouldn't the storm have disrupted Meervit's connection before that point? Could the two sisters have planned the whole thing? I didn't know the first thing about space weather, so there was no telling.

Whatever the truth, it had been Del, not Jexrah, who'd come to rescue me—and there was no doubt in my mind that Jexrah had been observing our interactions in some way—probably with a bug. *A simple night of stargazing*—but of course nothing with these rumae was ever simple.

"Do you need assistance back to your room?" Del asked me. I guess I looked shaky. With Jexrah in the room, though, it was a non-question that only allowed one answer.

"I'm fine, thanks," I told him and darted out the door before he could say a word otherwise.

Back in my suite, the walls were bare, Joanna lying low. I pitched my helmet into the corner, then shed my metal boots and the clinging catsuit. Midge had jumped off the bed to greet me, but she swiftly abandoned little old me for the far more interesting alien smells on my discarded clothing.

It had to be closing on midnight. Save for my breathing and Midge's snuffling, the room was silent. *All is calm, all is bright.* I was losing track of how many days I'd been on the ship; when was Christmas again? My poor dad. And I longed to be there with him in our little kitchen, a cinnamon-spiced candle burning, a pie on the sideboard, the meadow just outside our dinette window glistening with snow—but that would mean saying goodbye to the ship forever.

I slumped onto the bed. Was this what it felt like to be drawn and quartered? This place, and the alien living in it, had worked its way under my skin. I tried to picture myself going back—spending my days working in the shop, having girls' nights with Molly, sleeping in my little bedroom with wallpapered walls that didn't talk. Sometime in the future, a man, my husband, who I would tell—nothing about my time off Earth, of course. How could I?

Maybe flipping through my botanical drawings of the hothouse sometimes, to prove to myself that I hadn't dreamed it all up.

I had to believe that, if I did get to go home, an essential part of me would be changed forever. A whiff of otherworldliness, an indefinable aura—something vaguely foreign. Something alien.

I could feel myself drawn to Del like a moth to a flame. And if it were the case that I would already be returning home a different version of the person I'd been before… then going home with charred wings on top of that wasn't much different.

"Del… is back downstairs now?" I whispered to the open air.

"Yes," said Joanna softly.

"And is Jexrah with him?"

"She's in her suite. Turning in for the night, looks like."

"He's awake, though? Can I see him?"

"Now seems a safe time."

I slid off the bed and donned a T-shirt and leggings. Then, sock-footed, I walked the familiar route to the elevator, feeling strangely outside myself, like I wasn't the one doing the walking—as if perhaps an invisible thread around my waist was tugging me insistently onward.

I had to see him. That truth thrummed in my veins, loudly, over and over again. I had to see him. I had to see him, and all this might be resolved.

The elevator spirited me downward in seconds, and I

stepped out into the main room. He wasn't there, the room quiet as that night Joanna had wakened me. Then movement, the door across the way sliding open to reveal shadows on shadows. I squinted, searching for the lines of his silhouette.

"You came," he said quietly, and I nodded, for once not certain what to say. The thread around my navel cinched tighter, and I drifted forward a few more steps.

He emerged from the darkness. He was back in his usual getup of the chest strap and loose black trousers, and he looked haggard. I remembered how wild his eyes had been when he'd shouted at me in the pod.

"How was it with my sister?" he asked me. His voice was steady, but something in the way he was looking at me said that he was just as uncertain in this moment as I was.

I took it he meant Meervit, since any idiot could see how things stood between me and the other sister. "Fine. We talked—I think it was good. And the northern lights were amazing to see, before... before."

He nodded but didn't reply. Silence slumped in around us. I remembered that it had been I who'd squirmed out from under him and fled the room with nary an explanation. That would be a blow for anyone, human or otherwise.

"It was too much all at once," I said, trying to give him the truth, even if it had to be a barebones version of it. "I mean earlier, when we..."

He grimaced a little. "It's understandable."

"Maybe. But I'm sorry. And I'm sorry that I frightened you back there in the pods." I walked over to one of the lounge chairs, sat down. He took a seat across from me, with the techy ottoman between us, which a part of me definitely didn't like. I fidgeted. "Your sisters seem to care about you quite a lot."

"To excess, one might say."

It hadn't sounded that way from my talk with Meervit, but maybe that was just me, an only child, who'd always thought dimly how nice it would be to have a brother or sister. Though I'd never really daydreamed having sisters like his. "So what happens from here?" I asked. "Will they stay a while longer? When's the investigation over?"

He waggled his head back and forth a little, what I'd come to know as something like the rumae version of a shrug. "Several more days, perhaps."

"And how much longer will *we* be staying?"

"I am the vra-khinahar, and they merely khindrae. The most they can do is suggest it's time I return to the planet, no more."

"Your mother—?"

"—Will wait a while longer before making any official requests. It is her way." An undercurrent ran through that last sentence; he didn't entirely agree with the way his mother ran things, if I had to guess. Well, what son would?

"But we'll have to head back to Tenctah at some point," I said softly. "Sometime soon, I'm sure."

He bowed his head—this a motion common to both my species and his. Yes, we would leave Earth soon.

"We never did explore the rest of the river," I said, looking toward the sim room with a pang of sadness. I'd wanted to see the other fork, to sail under its beautiful overhanging boughs, and to do all that *with him*—and of course there might be time we could find in the days ahead, but that possibility looked more and more remote. This felt like a closing between him and I, though here we were still on the ship, still on Earth.

He didn't say anything, but I could see him looking at me from the corner of my eye. A question hung in the air. It was very late by now, but after the events of the last few hours I doubted I'd ever sleep again.

Then, in the very same second…

"Do you want to—?"

"We could—"

I gave a half laugh. "Yes," I said. I could feel a flush rising in my cheeks.

"You're sure?"

I rose and walked around the ottoman until I stood before him. I felt light-headed, me looking down at him and him up at me, almost like I'd drunk a glass or two of champagne. Yes, this one last time—it felt meant to be.

"I'm sure," I said, taking both his hands in mine. I could see the shadows in his eyes fall away again, and my soul floated higher.

He stood up, and his height, his closeness—dizzying. And though it was just our hands touching, even so I could remember just how it felt when my body pressed against his, and a sudden shyness stole over me, to stand before this… this *man*—and not a man, of course, but there was no other way for me to think of him… Not as a creature or a beast, because those terms were so harsh, nearly monstrous, and not as an alien, because that was too strange and cold, but as a person and a man, full-blooded, different-looking than me or any other human, but a man all the same.

And what was more natural than a man and a woman stealing a bit of time to be in each other's company?

Chapter Nine

I WAS EFFICIENT AT THE SIM-ROOM PREP, THIS NOW THE THIRD time I'd done this. Del left for a minute to change into clothes that would allow more nanobot contact, and I took the time to strip down to just my bra and panties, leaving the rest of my clothes on the couch. Then I entered the sim room and got into dust-me pose. Without even a voice command the ceiling showered me with shimmering particulate—Joanna's doing, I'm sure.

"Thanks," I breathed, and the corners of the room blushed pale pink.

Del came in, bare-chested as usual save for the strap, his longer pants exchanged for a style mid-thigh length. Whenever I saw him like this it was never so obvious how powerful he was, physically, and how physically *attractive*—yes, I could admit that now. Unbidden, the image came to me again of him shouting at me in the pod, and it made me weak-kneed.

He'd paused just past the doorway, taking in my own clothing change. I resisted the urge to squirm, the feel of his eyes on me deliciously unsettling. Of course, Del had seen me in similar garb—who could forget the *but-it's-Alexander-MCQUEEN* swimsuit?—but this felt different somehow, the significance of a first time and a last time rolled into one.

At last his gaze fell to the rubbery gray floor at my feet, its surface smudged with gold, then bounced to the side of the room, where Joanna's shadow still hid in the corner. "Ah," he said, before banishing her with a muttered phrase. Just the two of us now.

He quickly went through the motions of getting his own gold-dust treatment, then fetched the goggles from the hidden panel in the wall. Putting them on, I was back immediately on the riverbank, the sky above that the glowing, even blue of just past sunset. The air still held a lingering warmth from the day's heat, and I could feel the stress of the day shedding off as my muscles relaxed.

Del gave a quiet command from beside me, and I turned my head, blinked. There were no kayaks this time, but instead a boat with a flat, raft-like floor wide enough for the two of us, crafted from a reddish wood polished to a silky luster. Even in the fleeing light the boat shone like a tiger's eye stone.

"One of our traditional boats," Del explained as I brushed my hand lightly over the bow.

"She's beautiful." No other word for it.

He got in first before helping me aboard. There were no seats—instead the floor of the boat was spread with lush rugs and pillows. No oars, either. "How do you sail it?" I asked, then started a little when I felt a hum kick in below us. Without Del even raising a finger, the boat began a smooth journey down the river.

"A traditional boat?" I asked, raising an eyebrow.

"Traditional with a few additions."

He took a seat on one of the pillows, and I followed his lead, sitting beside him. I took a minute to admire the scenery gliding past us. The banks on either side of us were thick with more of those southern trees—white crape myrtles and orange trees heavy with fruit. They tinged the freshness of the air with a faint floral and citrus perfume.

"What's her name?" I asked with a nod to the boat as I came back to myself.

He looked at me askance. "What?"

"Oh, humans name their boats. Just like they would a spaceship." *Like the* Huivnarrut, I almost said, but caught myself just in time, not wanting to voice the sad name of Del's ship. I thought of it as cursed.

"What sort of names?" he asked with interest, not seeming to notice.

"Well, there are all different types of names. *Serenity, Liberty, The Pearl.* Or awful puns. Or many times people will pick a female name, after a wife or a mother."

He was quiet for a bit, thinking about that. Then... *"Beauty?"* he asked, eyes on me. "Is that a fitting name?"

I felt another wave of that tipsy-on-champagne feeling. "Very fitting," I said, stammering a little.

"Then that shall be her name."

We kept up our gentle course down the river. The myrtle

and orange trees petered out, replaced by mighty, craggy oaks. Those closest to the water seemed to sense their brethren on the opposite bank, their top boughs stretching to nearly meet high over our heads, shrouding us in a tunnel of leaves and branches. A warm flicker of light from the side caught my eye: a firefly. And there, a little ways away, another, then another.

"They're bugs," I told Del when I saw him looking on curiously. "Fireflies. Or some people call them lightning bugs."

One of them flashed between us, and Del caught it gently in his hand. A few seconds later it glowed again, illuminating the space between his fingers.

"Why do they glow?" he asked, as he opened his palm to let the firefly free.

"Sort of a beacon, I think. To, er, attract a mate." Goodness gracious.

"Some species on Tenctah use similar techniques," he said.

"Do they?"

"Of course. Smells, noises, various displays. Some understandable, some incomprehensible."

I nodded; getting it on was universally important, no doubt about that. A thought pulsed in my mind, a bit unformed. "Let me ask you something," I started tentatively. "I've been thinking, since I've spent so much time in the hothouse on the ship, with the plants… and with what you've showed me of Tenctah… and"—I hesitated to say it, then just plowed ahead—"rumae themselves… Well, it's all very similar, isn't it? Earth and Tenctah. And… humans and rumae. You could have had tentacles or an exoskeleton. You could have been twenty feet tall—or six inches tall! Or a—a sentient gas, or... I don't know." I shook my head, thinking of the conversation I'd had with Evan in the shop, just a day or two before I'd come aboard the ship. That night felt so long ago now, but I remembered his words well—how there were so many stars and planets and galaxies, and all it took was one species out of the morass of billions to make contact. I was no expert, but adding similarity of species into the equation had to be an order of magnitude more complex. That sort of thinking, the sheer odds of it all, was enough to make me dizzy. Was enough, even, to make me start thinking about God.

I looked over at Del, really looked at him. The steady, patient way he returned my gaze sent a spark down my spine. "But you're not any of that," I finished. "You're *you*."

Hard to believe he could have made any sense out of my blabbering, but he was nodding, his expression intent. "There are many species like that you mention," he said. "With... tentacles and the rest. The universe teems with life of every variety, creatures monstrous, humble, or unknowable. And their worlds differ just as much.

"But—" His voice faltered. "I was in search of a place to rest, and to think." Skirting around the awful events in Dru Gham—did he suspect his sister had told me what had happened? "And," he said, "I thought at the time that a similar place... with its qualities just a few shades different from my own home... might be restful. Peaceful. Earth was conveniently located, from where I was before this, but it was also the sort of place that seemed to extend an invitation. I can't imagine that a planet of sentient gases would feel so comfortable. But here, with the mountains, and the snow… and the colors of the sky, and the trees…" I felt a swell of pride at his word. There was no denying that my little corner of the globe could take your breath away.

"So," he continued, "I could have gone elsewhere. But it didn't happen that way."

"Like attracts like," I said, head swimming.

"Just so."

I liked that. I liked to think that perhaps some other variation of these events was playing itself out elsewhere, galaxies away—a different sort of girl, maybe with tentacles and maybe without, sitting beside her tempting shipmate.

Star-crossed—it was an unlucky word, right? Reserved for ill-fated pairings, the Romeos and Juliets of the world. But something about the term sparked an image in my mind that wasn't sad, but hopeful. Couldn't you imagine two shooting stars from opposite ends of the universe, beating their two, separate, lonely paths through cold, cold space? Only, with time, for them to draw nearer, their paths weaving around each other, touching, colliding.

Two shooting stars… or a girl on Earth and an alien in a ship.

So I did what had to be done—what *I* needed to be done—which was to kiss him again. He made to say something after the first few surprised seconds, but I stopped him, brushing my fingers to his lips as I said, "Please." And I'd never been more certain of anything, every ounce of me as calm as the waves softly lapping against the sides of our boat.

After that he didn't say a word, just kissed me, long and deeply. He was making more of those low, happy noises (I guess I was probably making some noises of my own), and the sound of him set me ablaze. His hands were all over me: the nape of my neck, my lower back, then, so very gently through the thin fabric of my bra, my breasts. I nearly cried out when one of his hands traveled lower to my leg, his thumb rubbing soft circles on my inner thigh. Sensation was building to a critical point, and not an atom within me stuttered.

"Bed," I gasped, just when it felt like I was about to go up in flames, and he made an approving back-of-the-throat growl before swooping me up in his arms like I was featherlight. The river scenery around us evaporated, depositing us back in the square sim room; in a few strides he was at the door, moving quickly toward the bedroom. He muttered something in Ziryahshun, and there was a flicker of movement in my peripheral vision. The corners of the walls now held only ordinary gray shadows. He'd revoked Joanna's privileges to the rest of his quarters, just like he'd dismissed her from the sim room.

He laid me on the bed, and I shimmied out of my bra and panties in two seconds flat. He took off his clothes too, even the always present chest strap, and after he was done he stood beside the bed for a moment, just looking. I returned his gaze before letting my eyes wander downward to drink in the strange beauty of him. The definition of his chest and arms, with muscles that flowed and cut into each other differently than a human man's would—but with a strong elegance that made my breath catch. The ruddy brown of him, which deepened to a richer red color at his groin. He had no balls—or they were internal, maybe. I'd never gotten around to picking up an anatomy book about the rumae. His cock, though, was very much present, and very much erect. It was the only hairless part of his body; the head, while still rounded, was a bit flatter than a human's, and the length curved slightly upward. But the overall shape was unmistakable—long and thick, but not obscenely so.

I found I couldn't bear just looking up at him any longer, and I tugged him down to join me. I had my arms around him, running my hands over his shoulders, his powerful back, and he—had me everywhere now, owning me with his hands, a finger stroking between my legs as his other hand teased my nipple. I moaned and rubbed against him, even as I tried to keep my head enough to explore him, too. He loved it when I stroked his cock with my fingers or held it firm. I stored these gleanings away for fun, future reference. And what about…? I shifted my position, so I could lick— His head jerked back, eyes half-shuttered, and I'd never been so happy.

Then he flipped me on my back before I could tease him further, his leg nudging my knees apart. I was aching for him, could feel the warm, hard presence of him there, poised to enter me, and the entire world dwindled down to that one point.

"Yes?" he asked hoarsely in my ear. *Yes*—I wrapped myself around him and pulled him into me.

His first strokes were cautious, not wanting to hurt me. There was an awful lot of him, and we kissed as I settled, shifted a little, took the rest of him in. Slowly we found a rhythm, which soon became less slow. He was paying a great deal of attention to my breasts, and I puzzled at that for a second before I made the connection and gave a throaty little laugh.

He moved back up to kiss me after a little while—a harder sort of kiss, near bruising my lips—and I arched my back, the feel of him filling me an almost painful ecstasy. Nothing existed now but Del, just him, and I could feel him tense as I got close, closer, and cried out. A few moments later he thrust into me hard, gave a grating cry to echo mine, and became an unmoving statue above me, sheathed to the hilt, every muscle in stark, flexed relief. I watched him, awed and waiting for whatever came next. Then I realized with a start that there was movement down below—a rapid pulsing in his cock that went on longer than I'd expected—fifteen seconds, maybe. I convulsed around him, moaning a little, and at last he stirred and seemed to come back to himself.

We shared a long look. He still had me pinned, and I expected him to slide out—to give a yawn, perhaps, then to hold me to his chest as we fell asleep.

But Del was a rumae, not a human. Shifting his gaze from me to look around the room, he opened his mouth and loosed another cry—but no, *cry* wasn't strong enough a word. A roar. It was a wrenching, primal, shocking noise—a challenge to the world that vibrated through my bones. His gaze was darting side to side, his upper body set in a way that meant business, and I could well imagine him leaping off me to do battle with some invisible foe.

But there was no one there, of course, and after a moment he relaxed, though he looked a little bewildered.

"Okay?" I asked him softly, reaching up to caress his cheek, and he looked at me, eyes still clouded with wildness. "Okay?" I repeated.

He seemed to hear me that time and gave me a sharp, strange nod. Then his lips crooked upward into a smile, and he withdrew at last. I gave a tiny gasp at the sudden absence of him, though a pleasant, wet warmth remained between my legs. I was drunk with pleasure, drowsiness pressing on my brain, and when he lay down beside me I nestled into him, exploring the shape of his arm, the build of his legs, the feel of his pelvis against my hip. We were puzzle pieces from two different pictures that somehow fit snugly, perfectly.

We fell asleep like that, tangled together.

Chapter Ten

I WOKE A WHILE LATER—A SLOW, LAZY AWAKENING. DEL HAD me tucked tightly into his chest, the musk of his spicy, male scent like a whole other embrace. He was still sleeping, his even breath a tickle on my neck.

Warm contentment purred within me, and I closed my eyes again with a soft, happy sigh.

Sometime later still—minutes? An hour? It was all a haze. He was awake, his hand cupping my breast, squeezing it gently, then using his finger to trace slow circles around my nipple. He paused when he felt it stiffen at his touch; he was learning me.

I pressed into him, letting him know I was awake. I wasn't the only one with something stiff right now.

"These are delightful," he said into my ear, both hands at my breasts now. "Our women do not have these…"

"Breasts," I finished for him. "Or boobs. Or tits."

"Tits," he said slowly, trying the word on for size. "I like that one best." And he kept playing with my nipple with the one hand, while the other found its way between my legs, exploring me there. His lips he pressed to the nape of my neck, kissing me, licking me, until I was quivering, my desire a wound only he could heal.

He waited until I came, shaking in his arms, then took me hard from behind. I knew I would ache the next day—*wanted* to ache, to feel the evidence of our time together, even if he was somewhere else.

When he came I was prepared for his prolonged stillness, the insistent throb of his cock as he spent himself into me, his final, possessive bellow. I wasn't prepared for the feeling that came over me.

It was a feeling that said *stay*. Not just now, for this one night, but forever. I'd felt the glimmerings of such thoughts, but now the urge, the *compulsion*, crashed over me. I could stay with him, as his—lover? Partner? I'd destroy the gunpowder and do whatever necessary to prove myself trustworthy of returning to Earth sometimes. Appeal the rumae laws that forbade me to return; surely Del could help with that, as vrakhinahar. Then go with him to Tenctah and travel back to Earth occasionally, using what they called snap travel. I resolved to discuss my plan with him in the morning, sans any mention of the gunpowder. That secret would die with me.

"You're thinking of something?" he asked, pulling me into the crook of his arm again.

"Later," I said, my cheek on his chest. He was so solid, so

warm. "Let's just stay like this." Being here with him right now, in the dark, private cave of this room, felt like a moment suspended in time. Discussing plans and practicalities would break the spell.

He made a pleased noise deep in his chest and hugged me in closer. "Then tell me something you haven't told me before. About yourself."

"We'll trade?"

"Yes."

"All right." I thought for a moment. I knew he didn't want frivolous little details. "Well," I said finally, "I can tell you about my house." It was something I was proud of, how my family's prospector history had been hammered into the creaking wood and old nails of the farmhouse. So I narrated to him the story as it had been narrated to me as a child, about my Polish great-great-great-granddad, the gold he'd found, the widow he'd married, then I described our house itself to him in broad strokes.

"You said your family has multiple residences?" I asked, peering up at him. "Besides the great house in Ohruhn?"

His eyes slid to somewhere far away. I wished I could see whatever he was seeing. "Yes. My favorite is a place we keep quiet, where it's easier to stay out of the public eye. It's necessarily secluded by nature. I have many happy memories of visiting there when I was younger. Now I do not get the opportunity to visit it often—perhaps once yearly. One of our years."

"How long is that?" I asked, sitting up a bit. I had never even considered such a thing. There was so much I didn't know.

"Something like… one and a third of your years."

Well, that wasn't so different. But on the topic of years… "So how old are you?"

"Forty-one."

I did some quick mental math and started. "That would make you fifty-something! On Earth."

"Correct. Though I'm still considered to be in my youth. I understand that a fifty-year-old on Earth is middle-aged."

"How long—?"

He anticipated my question. "Most rumae nowadays live until they are at least a hundred and thirty. A hundred and sixty isn't unheard of."

"That's… God." I shook my head, trying to do the conversion. "Two hundred years old? Something like that?"

"Approximately. I've shocked you. Corinne—"

"More surprised than shocked," I said, tracing a line along one of his ribs with the tip of my finger. How lovely it sounded when he said my name—that slight emphasis on the *R* somehow sensual. "Here, I should tell you something." But when I cast my mind out for inspiration, nothing came back. It seemed to me that I lived a simple life—a simple, *short* life—compared to him.

"What of your earlier life?" he asked after a moment's pause. "When you were in… school." Right—he'd mentioned before how the rumae used some sort of apprenticeship system for their schooling, dissimilar to our educational system.

Apprenticeships… My mind stalled on that word for half a

second, coupling the thought with everything Meervit had related to me.

He could tell me all the details in time, once he was ready. "Well, I was a happy kid," I said in answer to his question. "I mean, until Mom died. I didn't like school that much—thought it was boring. But my grades were decent enough, and I got along with the other kids okay, and the teachers liked me, too, even though they could tell my heart wasn't in it. I just wanted to be outside, playing. Or gardening—that comes from my mom." Sleepiness was coaxing me to ramble. It had to be into the wee hours of the night by now, or maybe even drawing on towards dawn. "She loved plants, and I took care of our garden after she died. That's why I thought to study botany when I started college. But—" I bit off my sentence. This was a sore spot for me still, something I hadn't fully reckoned with.

"I guess I just didn't like the bookwork in college. A few of the classes were fine, I guess." Here I was thinking of Professor Thoner and his explosives fixation. "But I didn't like most of my classes. If a plant is growing, that's living proof of a lot of incredible things, right? That the soil is good, the amount of water, the temperature, the sunlight. Reading about it on a page took the magic out of it. And..." I frowned, wrestling with my thoughts. "In a way, taking those classes felt like losing my mom a second time. Because she'd never needed to know the ins and outs of the—the vascular system for her to grow plants. She just knew how to do it, and then she taught me."

I curled closer into him, his chest soft as suede against my cheek. His heartbeat had a different rhythm than mine.

"You've spent a great deal of time in the hothouse since you've been here," he said after a while.

"I've been studying the plants. Cleaning things up a bit." That and other activities that I would destroy the evidence of come morning.

"I've stayed away," he said. "Purposefully. From what Joanna told me, it seemed like a place you might wish to keep private."

I looked up at him again. "I want you to see it. Maybe I can show you tomorrow. Now it's your turn." Misty gray shadows were starting to squirm at the corners of my vision—overtiredness—but I wanted to hold on to this moment with him, to savor it, like letting a piece of hard candy dissolve slowly on your tongue.

"My turn?"

"Tell me something."

"I see. I… enjoy music."

"Really?" I asked, pushing myself up on one elbow the better to see him. Something tugged my attention away from him for a second; the corner where the mangled mirror had stood before was now empty. I refocused on Del. "What do you mean— you enjoy listening to music? Do you sing?"

"Mainly the former. That was why… I enjoyed your musical summons quite a lot." He eyed me. "Despite some of your questionable selections."

"There is nothing questionable about AC/DC and Björk. But what sort of music do you like? You should sing something!"

He was giving me a look that told me he was halfway sorry for sharing this information. "I'm not overly skil—"

"Oh, I don't care about that." I wasn't going to let him get out of this. "I can't even imagine what rumaean—rumaean?—music is like."

"There's quite a large breadth of it."

I gave him my best puppy-dog eyes. "Then sing something from *your* childhood. You all must have nursery rhymes? Or lullabies?"

A pause. "Yes." I maintained a steadfast silence. "All right," he said, his arm settling me against him.

And in a halting voice, which steadied after a few seconds, he sang for me. The song wasn't so neatly ordered as the human lullabies I knew, the cadence alternately slow then lilting. It took a while for me to grasp the meandering melody, and the words, of course, were a wholesale mystery. Yet in his low, rumbling voice the song was beautiful, and it spun a spell of sweet melancholy around us. I would ask him what it meant when it was over…

But the song had done its job, a proper lullaby that ushered me back to sleep. In a later dream haze, I remembered him lifting me from the bed and bringing me back upstairs. A grand lady being gently transported by litter. A groom carrying his bride across the threshold. Happy—I was so happy.

When I woke, I was in my own bed, and he was gone.

Chapter Eleven

I BROUGHT MY HANDS TO MY FACE, TRIED TO RUB AWAY MY disorientation, looked around the room again. Midge was snoozing beside me, and there was no sign of Del.

Last night had been real, hadn't it? I brought a hand between my legs, feeling tentatively, and a pleasant soreness bloomed. No, I hadn't dreamed it all up.

"Hey there," I murmured to Midge, playing with the black silk of her fur. "Well, what do you think about all of that?" She cocked an ear at me and rolled over for belly rubs. Any lingering scent of sin on me wasn't too interesting, I guess.

I daydreamed through my morning routine, memories of the night before never far away. No denying that a night of good—great—fantastic—sex had me feeling satiated as a cat with a bellyful of warm milk.

Joanna was all pinks and purples and champagne golds, obviously over the moon. Del might have banished her from the bedroom, but it didn't take a genius to deduce that we'd slept together, and Joanna was, in fact, a certified genius. I'm sure she also felt mightily pleased with herself; it wasn't like she hadn't been doing her best to set the stage for romance.

The rest of the day I spent normally enough, though I was always floating on my cloud of dreamy satisfaction. I played with Midge, did some pruning, read a few chapters of *Emma* with Joanna, then continued our mystery game with Nadia Spires, amateur sleuth/professional organizer. I'd uncovered that it was a good thing Nadia hadn't hooked up with the rattlesnake-tattooed bartender—not only did he help keep the town's residents liquored up, but he also dealt coke and molly.

"I do have one question," I said to Joanna, apropos of nothing, when a sudden, terrifying possibility hurtled through me. "The khindrae's suite—is it, er, far away from Del's bedroom…?" Because if he'd been able to hear the boombox from my room above, then there was a distinct chance she'd heard some of the… commotion… downstairs.

"She's two floors above, on the opposite end," she answered smoothly.

"Oh, good," I said, breathing easily again. "That's lucky."

"Yes, lucky indeed," she said, glowing gold with pride before shifting back to a peony pink. Sneaky, sneaky.

One thing I didn't do that day was destroy the gunpowder. In the light of day, it had occurred to me that it was crucially important to talk with Del first about if it were even possible to work out a plan where I saw him off and on, shuttling between Earth and Tenctah. I also wanted to have a serious talk with myself about whether I was truly prepared to undertake the world's longest long-distance relationship.

I was thinking the answer was yes. Still, it was a big decision.

But Del was busy, Joanna said, with his sisters and his vra-khinahar duties. "He can't spare an hour?" I asked after dinner that night. Just one hour, to talk things over with him and perhaps still have time for other activities. Plus I didn't like going a whole day without seeing a single other living being besides my dog.

"I'm afraid it wouldn't fit his schedule," Joanna said apologetically. "But Khindrae Jexrah has proposed a dinner tomorrow—herself, Khindrae Meervit, the master, and yourself. Do you wish to accept the invitation?"

"That's fine." I wouldn't be able to talk to him with Jexrah present, but at least I'd be able to see him.

With a while left before I'd head to bed, I ran myself a bath with extra bubbles and had fun imagining Del coming in to join me. When I came out of the bathroom, all soft, pruney, and nice-smelling, something was up with Joanna—she wasn't as chatty, and the pinks and lavenders had ceded to a poor butterscotch imitation of her basic apricot.

"Something wrong?" I asked.

"No, no," she said, squirming, and her coloring lightened to a creamy mustard. Whatever—with royal siblings on board, I'm sure she had a lot to deal with. If it didn't involve me, I was happy to keep basking in memories of the night before.

Which I did, falling asleep remembering how it had felt to lie in Del's arms.

The next day I spent much like the last, in isolation save for Midge and Joanna. She still looked a little off, and I didn't ask. Truth be told, I didn't see Joanna for a good portion of the day;

the sex glow had faded, leaving a hunger in its place, so I threw myself into work in the hothouse as a distraction. There was a ferocious overgrowth of weeds choking out some luminescent, snowdrop-like flowers, so I took an hour to pull those out. Next I lugged over the weed corpses and some more accumulated plant waste to a corner I'd cleared to make way for a compost heap. I'd have to start collecting my leftover food scraps to feed the process.

That done, I grabbed my sketchbook and made some drawings of several new species I'd noticed. I'd filled half the book's pages already with my amateur botanical cataloging, as well as a few full-page sketches of some of my favorite parts of the room. Maybe I'd do another one of those now... I sat down right in the middle of the stone path and committed a grove of young saplings to paper, until my back was aching.

Anything to get my mind off the urge to see him.

Also, I was doing my best to forget about the clod of gunpowder currently drying in the gohrrow husk, not fifty feet away from me.

Finally I called it a day and plodded back to my room to take a bath. This time I didn't luxuriate; all I could think of was the upcoming dinner, of seeing him for the first time since our night together.

When I came out of the bathroom, Joanna had prepared a marigold-yellow silk gown for me, with a cowl neck, thin straps, a low, sweeping back, and a slit a few inches shy of scandalous. The whisper-thin silk traced my silhouette, dripping down like molten gold to pool on the floor in a short train.

"Not too much?" I asked, skimming a hand over the material. This was the finest thing I'd ever worn, bar none.

"Not at all," Joanna said. She was looking peachier; if anything could drag her out of her weird funk, it would be clothes. "Now try the shoes."

The heels she'd fabricated for me were more sculpture than shoe: a cream-colored heel inlaid with golden lilies, bronze vines twining around the top of the shoe to lace me in. Tiny pink jewels—morganite?—studded the vines here and there, catching the light at odd angles.

"Who designed these?" I asked, putting on my morganite necklace to match. "Alexander McQueen again?"

She tutted. "No, no, not this time. It's all my own design. Just what I thought would suit you best."

I looked in the mirror, sucked in a breath. I had all the filters off, but this was a form of magic spun not from technology but clever seams and flawless craftsmanship. In this outfit I was a different woman—taller, glowing, ready to be whisked away in my limo to the Academy Awards, or perhaps a royal ball.

"You're sure?" I asked Joanna again in a quieter voice, thinking now of how I would look to Del. And, for that matter, to his sisters. There was no hiding in this dress.

"You're having dinner with the two khindraes and the vra-khinahar," she said. "They're royalty."

"I don't want to upstage—"

"It could never be too much," she said firmly, and that was that.

We were to dine in a room one floor up. I made my way

upstairs and took a deep breath before I pushed the button to enter, preparing myself. A faint perfumed smell filtered through the door. Incense: this was to be a formal rumae meal.

All right, time to do this. In my peripheral vision I could see Joanna quivering with purple anticipation as I squared my shoulders and went inside.

They'd picked a room on the smaller side, with a lavishly set table. The many small dishes were enough to feed an army, though it would be just us three dining. Unexpectedly, music filled the air—a slower, alien music with humming chords right on the edge of atonality.

A shimmer from above caught my eye, and I tipped my head back. On the ceiling, where I'd normally expect to see glimmerings of Joanna, was instead projected a golden, moving menagerie of beasts unknown to me. The detail was exceptional: predators' fangs snapped at doe-eyed prey; majestic, hunchbacked animals moved steadily as a herd; sharp, aquatic-looking creatures whizzed around the edges.

I could have watched the projection all day, but I brought my attention to the three siblings, already assembled. Jexrah and Del were dressed in what I took to be formal clothes: her in a chartreuse, frothy, tulle-like concoction and him in a dressier version of his usual chest strap and trousers. Meervit was perched on a prettily carved stand beside the table, so that she wouldn't have to hover all throughout dinner.

Del was by a side table in the corner, facing away from me as he fiddled with something, so it was the two sisters who saw me first. Jexrah gave me a bemused smile, and Meervit's red orb eye glowed brighter. I shivered. I had a few suspicions about what had happened the other night in the escape pod; to my mind, it looked more likely than not that one or both of them had halfheartedly tried to kill me.

"Welcome," Jexrah said, as Del continued to mess with whatever he was doing in the corner. "You can sit here." She indicated the seat between herself and Meervit. Lovely.

Del turned around then, some sort of shiny violet bauble in his hand, and saw me. I could see the moment his countenance shifted, the princely veneer briefly cracking. There was a want in his eyes as he took me in, and an intoxicating heat sparked under my skin as his gaze traveled from my eyes down to my lips, then skirted lower still to my breasts, my hips.

All this in just a second, before his face tightened and he showed the purple trinket in his hand to Jexrah. "This is one by—" Here he said something growly in Ziryahshun. The side table beside him was littered with many more such baubles, all in shining jewel tones.

"Ah, he's very talented," Jexrah said and took the object from him. I saw now that it was a little, glassy cylinder; she popped the top of the cylinder off, and the menagerie above us evaporated, replaced by thousands of sharp, silvery blades of grass. A breeze carved patterns in the field, the grass blades bobbing in tandem.

"The ampoules contain bottled artscapes," Meervit explained in her thin drone voice. "Commissioned from Tenctah's most skilled artists. Each artscape can be used but one time only—an ephemeral pleasure."

So I was to never see the golden menagerie again—I felt a small stab of sadness. "It's very beautiful," I said, with an upward nod at the dancing blades of grass. The wind was knitting the blades together into intricate patterns, the field suddenly a knotted, living quilt.

"You can open one yourself later, if you'd like," Del said to me—not with any special tenderness, but as a host would speak to a guest.

"Sure," I replied, feeling unsteady, and trained my gaze on the food. The small dishes and plates filling the table appeared to be color-coded and laid on the table in some sort of deliberate order. Red plates, blue plates, green plates, and a few scattered coppery ones as well. Surely I was smart enough to figure this out. Something squirmed on a blue dish at the far end of the table, and I tried to concentrate on that, on how gross that was. What I didn't want to think about was a relationship spent pretending, concealing, hiding. Him a host and me a guest. Him a prince and me a nobody.

Don't think about it. Take a seat. Look at the plates and puzzle over all these odd things to eat.

Don't think about it.

We ate dinner. The meal was subdued—unremarkable, even. The three rumae chatted mostly in English, for my benefit, and the conversation floated from topic to topic, never landing on anything solid. Partway through Jexrah pressed me to pick a new artscape. *(Poke the monkey so we can see it do a trick!)* I chose an emerald-hued ampoule, uncapped it, and a dense cloud of glimmering vapor appeared above our heads.

There were hidden figures sneaking through the mist, it seemed to me, their silhouettes just barely obscured. It was an uneasy sight—certainly not anything to inspire an appetite.

Del, too, was making me uneasy. Not because he was keeping a tight lid on anything that would indicate more than a host-guest relationship—that was only to be expected, after all—but because… I couldn't put my finger on it. Something else seemed to lurk in his expression whenever he looked my way. Which he was doing at every possible opportunity.

I was flattered, of course. It was a very pretty dress. But something was wrong; I could feel it in the air. And I thought of Joanna's strangeness these past two days, and I wondered…

By the meal's end the color-coded plate system was just as much a mystery to me, and whatever was up with Del was still a mystery, too.

"Would you care to join us for some maht?" Jexrah asked me, and a server bot scuttled out of the corner with a tall white cylinder and three small cups.

"That's alcoholic?" I asked her.

"She's never had maht!" Jexrah cried, looking gleefully at her siblings. Then back to me: "Oh, but you have to try it." (*Let's see the monkey walk on two legs!*)

"I'm not sure—"

"Just a sip or two. It comes from a fruit called—it would translate to something like *berry of youth*. This vintage has the highest certification, straight from the Eelagov croplands," she said. "None of that fabricated swill."

"Well, in that case," I said, fed up with her, and reached for the already full cup in front of me. Trust the server bot to realize I was going to lose this argument.

"It's a drink to sip and savor," Meervit said, to help me out. Across the table, Del was looking at Jexrah stonily. He was angry with her, and, truth be told, I was getting angry with the both of them. Wouldn't it have been nice for him to stick up for me, to tell Jexrah where she could put her maht instead?

But he couldn't, I reminded myself for the hundredth time, not while he was the host and I just the guest. Which meant I had to deal with Jexrah the best I could.

I regarded the thin, brown, opaque liquid in the cup and took a gingerly sip.

It wasn't great, and that was a charitable description; *disgusting* might have been more apt. Essence of Granny Smith apples, but with the sourness turned up to eleven, and a bitterness suffusing the whole brew.

I knew Jexrah would have loved for me to gag and spit it out, and that knowledge was the only reason I forced a swallow. I could feel the progression as the maht slid down my throat and into my chest, not with a hard-liquor burn, but with the bite of battery acid.

Then I smiled broadly at her (hoping the maht hadn't eaten all my teeth to nubs). "That's really something." And I took another awful sip to prove the point.

Jexrah and Del drank from their cups as well, and I turned in my seat to face Meervit. "Sorry you can't have some yourself. Or any of the food, for that matter."

She shifted, her silver hardware gleaming. "It's really no issue. I'll dine once I de-link from the drone. My personal chef is quite exceptional."

"Is that so?" I said, my eyes straying back to the table as she started telling me all about him. The different-colored plates really were quite pretty, weren't they? Very *vivid*. Like we were dining off precious stones.

"You like the maht?" Jexrah asked from my other side, jerking my attention back to the conversation. The lemon-lime of her dress was fluorescent under the lights, so bright I expected it to start vibrating, and Jexrah was peering at me like the Cheshire Cat from the center of it all. That's how I felt right now, eating dinner with three aliens—like I was in Oz. No, silly, Oz was from *The Wizard of Oz*. The Cheshire Cat was from Wonderland.

Oh, Jexrah had asked me a question, hadn't she? Best not to ignore the khindrae—I'd learned *that* lesson.

"No, it's awful," I said, then blinked as my brain caught up with my mouth. I was feeling real bold all of a sudden.

Well, no matter—it wasn't like there was any affection to lose between myself and Del's sister. She hated me, I knew, and I wondered if that more came down to royal concern for Ailopt or sisterly protection of her brother. Of course, both were understandable. Admirable, even.

"You know, I'm not that bad," I said to her. "We could probably be friends, if we tried."

"But aren't we friends?" she asked, smiling. "At least cordial acquaintances."

Hm, perhaps we were. It was hard to form coherent thoughts right now. Across the table, Del said something reproachful to his sister in Ziryahshun. I scowled at him, since Jexrah and I were having a moment. Then a realization bowled me over, and I clutched at the table. (Almost spilled the remainder of my maht, but thankfully didn't. I was looking forward to another sip or two.)

"The plates make sense," I said excitedly. "The colors are for flavor types, aren't they? And you can mix and match—red with green or blue, copper with everything. That's genius."

"She's an interesting one, isn't she?" drawled Jexrah, looking to her brother, and I beamed at her. What a nice thing to say!

"*You're* real interesting," I said, flapping a hand at her. "I mean, look at that dress! Is that by Alexander McQueen?"

Next came individual moments of clarity, like a photo slideshow: Meervit making her excuses and buzzing from the room; me swirling the maht around and around in my cup; an artscape of riches above us, jewels afloat in a roiling sea of gold dust. Time stretched and contracted like a rubber band, back and forth, back and forth. Suddenly dinner was officially over, and I was rising from my chair, the ceiling descending in a rush to meet my head.

"Wonderland!" I think I said. "But I didn't take the Drink Me potion. Unless maht is like—ohh…"

Out in the hallway then, for years and years. There was somewhere I was trying to go, but damned if I knew where it was. My legs were heavy, each step Sisyphean. A lemon-lime voice laughed sharply, and a vermilion voice chastised the other into silence.

"But how do we *get* there?" I asked.

"It's really not far."

At least someone knew the way.

My feet of stone left me, bit by bit. The thoughts in my brain seemed more liable to stay put now. An orb light glowed overhead. Joanna loomed, all blue and worried and squirmy.

"Hey there," I said, waggling my fingers at her. "You need to chill out."

Skip ahead again, and I was in the corridor with Del, and we were alone, and he was looking *so good*. "No, you can't have any more," he said morosely. "This is exactly what Joanna suspected would happen, which is why I never offered you any. Sleep should help. A great deal of sleep. The maht will probably keep coming in waves."

"I don't want to sleep," I said, eyeing him up and down. "I want—"

"Almost there," he said, his hand on the small of my back to lead me down the hallway. He sounded weary, like we'd already been through this conversation.

"We should—"

"Here it is, just ahead," he said. My body felt cloud-like, buoyant. Good thing he was here, so warm and solid, to keep me from floating away.

Oh, we'd arrived! "Here we are," I trilled, and I darted into the room, tugging him along with me. Midge came over to say hi—Midge!—and the bed awaited us, wide and inviting, practically beckoning.

"No, Corinne," Del said. He'd dropped my hand, was standing close to the door like he was readying himself for an escape.

"But I've missed you," I said, frowning. "I haven't seen you for two days." The dress's delicate straps fell from my shoulders as I walked over to him, cool air caressing my skin. I wanted him to rip the whole thing off me, silken perfection be damned. I wanted to feel him again, how he'd filled me to the painful brink of pleasure.

So I walked back to him. I knew what would happen next, like I was gazing into a crystal ball: ever honorable, he'd let me steal one kiss, which would start off short and grow longer. I would feel him against me, ready, and I'd ache for him, lean into him, and even if he didn't lose control of himself then, at least I'd have that tantalizing memory to fall asleep to.

None of that happened, though. I made my way over to him, reached for him, and he jerked backwards.

"What—?"

"You need to rest."

"You're avoiding me," I said. Sparks flashed in my peripheral vision, unreality rearing its head. I fought to stay in the moment and not fall headfirst into the maht once more. "You slept with me, and now you're avoiding me."

He stilled. A buzzing was starting in my head, like a swarm of bees had taken nest in my skull. I said something else unkind to him, but I couldn't hear myself through the buzzing, and his answer went unheard, too.

The edges of the room were expanding outwards. Del was fading away into the distance, though his feet did not move.

I knew nothing after that.

IT WAS EVAN'S CLOSING-TIME TRADITION TO HEAD OUT BACK behind the shop to admire the Big D for a few minutes while he vaped. He maintained this tradition even in wintertime, despite the cold and the snow and the wind off the river. It made him feel like a settler of old, surveying the land before him with a mind to make it his own.

All the same, he thought tonight as he watched the chill river flow, lucky for Corinne to be down in Texas in the heat; it really was cold out here tonight. Her sudden departure had been a shock to everyone at the shop and had necessitated a decent amount of schedule rearranging to cover her shift, but good for her if that was what she needed. He'd texted her, obviously, but hadn't gotten a response. Neither had Molly, a crime deserving of capital punishment, to hear Molly talk about it. Well, it just backed up what Corinne's dad had told Ray, that she needed time away. Space or whatever. What Texas had to offer that Montana didn't was beyond Evan—but of course Corinne would come back eventually and tell them all about it.

The approaching crunch of boots on snow coming around the side of the shop was unexpected. Evan hastily slipped his pen back into his pocket.

"Gabriella told me you were out here."

It was Joe Gagnon—unexpected. Evan straightened up a bit. "Hey, Joe, what's up?"

The truth was that Joe wasn't looking his best; that was plain to see, even in the meager light afforded by the sole light bulb behind the shop. His dark hair had a slight greasy sheen to it, and the smile on his lips faded too quickly. He looked at Evan dead-on, not sparing a second's glance at the river.

"Nice night," Joe said.

"Sure is." If your definition of *nice* was a temperature cutting enough to freeze your balls off.

"You come out here every night?"

"Pretty much." Here Evan dug the pen out of his pocket again and offered it to Joe. The man looked like he needed it.

Joe shook his head though. "Thanks, but no. Wanted to ask you something real quick. I was just driving by…"

"Yeah, sure."

"Corinne hasn't texted you or anything, has she? Since she left?"

"No, nothing."

"But you did text her, right?"

It was just your standard weed-induced paranoia, surely… something about Joe's intonation… Evan felt a sudden, strong stab of apprehension. *Watch your words.*

"Yeah, just the once. I think everyone probably did. Just that… she didn't give notice."

"Right," Joe said. "Right. Well, she needs some time to herself. A break."

"Sure." *Break* was a funny word; half of the word *breakup*, and half its scope as well.

There was something to the way Joe was standing… He was very still. Very attentive. Poised. And—this was definitely the influence of the weed—everything else was moving. The wind lightly jostling tree branches… the slow, constant flow of the river… dark clouds sliding over sharp, bright stars.

Joe was the only thing holding still.

"So Gabriella and I are going out to the Roadhouse this weekend," Evan said. "Should be nice." A lie—Evan had been gathering his courage to ask her, but hadn't bit the bullet yet. He would after Joe left.

"Oh, yeah?"

"Mm."

An indefinable essence hung in the air. For a moment, all that could be heard was the frothing of the river. Then: "Nice," Joe said. "She seems like a real catch. Looks like it, anyway."

"Hopefully it works out."

"She didn't mention anything in there," Joe said, cocking his head toward the shop, unblinking.

Evan shrugged a little. "Yeah, well…"

"You and Gabriella," Joe said. "Hm. Well, good for you, man. I'll see you later."

"Later."

And just like that he left back the way he'd come, and Evan was alone again in the small spotlight cast by the light bulb.

An icy breeze from over the river caressed his cheek. It felt like the temperature had dropped ten degrees further.

Good that Corinne was in Texas, he thought again.

Chapter Twelve

I DRIFTED ON A VAST, BROWN SEA. SOMETIMES A COMFORTING voice reached through the haze, with words I didn't understand. Sometimes I felt the press of a hand to my forehead or cheek.

But mostly I stayed adrift.

Out on the ocean, I was thinking, in that strange, abstract way you do in dreams. Images came to me, washed toward me on the waves. Del's look of strained, shocked frustration after I'd tackled the val. The shop, which felt a million miles away by now, and all my friends in it: Molly, Evan, Ray. The soft way Del had looked at me when he'd christened the boat *Beauty*. My dad all alone, puttering sadly about our creaking farmhouse.

Del, home, Del, home… An unceasing loop, like a snake eating its own tail. And it started to seem to me that all of life was a bit like this, a push and pull, a give and take. Even the wealthiest among us, whether they're wealthy in riches or family or power, have things they long for.

Time was seeping in again, in dribs and drabs. A few seconds here, a moment there. I gathered that I was in bed, that Del was keeping a nighttime vigil beside me. I even caught a glimpse of him once, sitting in the blue armchair beside the bed. His eyes were far away somewhere, deeply pensive, his expression dark. I tried to find my mouth muscles, so I could say something to him…

Back out to sea I went.

It was a female voice that lured me back towards consciousness the next time. Joanna? But no, this accent wasn't British, but the familiar growl of Ziryahshun in translation.

She spoke to me in gentle, wheedling tones. Questions—a whole heap of them. I would have answered her, but the connection from my brain to my mouth again proved too shaky.

Then Del was there, angry. A back-and-forth, and the female speaker was gone. That was his sister, I remembered suddenly; she had something to do with me floating on this sea of brown.

When I came to next, I was attended by both Joanna and Del, in the middle of some sort of low, tense discussion in Ziryahshun. Joanna was plainly in comfort mode, and Del… he sounded despondent. My knowledge of their language close to nil, there was no saying what they were discussing.

The maht's influence was giving way. I bobbed in and out on the tide, my glimpses of consciousness more and more frequent, until, without me really knowing it had happened, that terrible, lifeless sea left me, like it had been sucked down a great storm drain.

I drew a breath, tested my jaw muscles. They chose to work this time. I opened my eyes.

I was alone, save for Joanna's bare shadow on the wall and Midge, huddled in next to me.

I took a moment to revel in reality. The bedsheets felt dirty, my head ached, the light was too bright for my tender eyes, and I was glad of all of that. I could put up with almost anything, if it meant having my mind back.

All right, time to make use of my jaw muscles. I'd never again take them for granted. "Joanna," I called.

She was there in an instant, and so began the process of let's-fuss-over-Corinne. How did I feel? Could I count up to twenty, then back down again? (I told Joanna yes, then gave her a dour-enough look that she moved on.) Was I able to sit up in bed? Or maybe it would be better to just lie there a bit, find my bearings…

I ignored that last part and sat up. Midge's tail wagged at my movement, and she got up and started washing my arm with her tongue. She wasn't wrong; I needed a bath, badly. My hair was a matted mess, and a thin layer of dried sweat coated my skin. Looking down, I saw I was still in the gold dress. Deep creases marred its smoothness, a musty smell rising from the fabric.

Then I thought a little more about my dog, still licking my arm, and felt a sharp surge of panic. "Wait, who's been—?"

"The master has been taking her for walks and feeding her," Joanna said. "He tried to play with her to give her some exercise, but she wouldn't leave your side."

I'd have to thank him for that—and apologize to him. I was sure there was a reason he wasn't here right now, and probably it had to do with the last thing I remembered saying to him.

With creaking care, I got out of bed to a chorus of protestations from Joanna. Probably it wasn't a good idea to push myself, but I felt that desperate convalescent's urge to work on being anything but sick.

"How long was I out?" I asked, stretching. I was achy all over.

"About two days. It's seven a.m."

Two days? "What day is it?"

There was an infinitesimal pause. "The twenty-fourth."

Christmas Eve. I closed my eyes, took a few steadying breaths. I'd never spent a Christmas apart from my dad before, and I was sad to start now.

But there was no help for it. "Do you think she knew what she was doing?" I asked to change the subject.

"Who?"

"Jexrah. With the maht."

"I'm not certain about that," Joanna said carefully.

"She was in here, wasn't she? Asking me questions while all my defenses were down."

"She snuck in once while the master was out with Midge. You should have seen how angry he was. But it turned out all right; you could hardly speak, let alone reveal anything compromising."

"She's evil," I said.

"She really might not have anticipated the maht would hit you so hard…"

"No. She's evil."

Joanna sighed, and I decided to drop it. Her (figurative) hands were tied by her loyalty to Del and, in turn, the royal family; she was never going to just come out and say, *Yeah, that was really fucked up*.

"How about breakfast?" I asked her, extending an olive branch. "Oh, and water."

Joanna made me a bowl of guvu, which sounds faintly horrid, but in actuality is similar to oatmeal. After that, I downed something like a gallon of water, then went into the bathroom to make myself into a real person again.

Thankfully there was no rush to be anywhere, as was always the case for me now, so I treated myself to the works: soaking in a bath for a good long while, easing the knots out of my hair, shaving, cutting my nails. Slowly, I felt more stirrings of strength. Food, water, cleanliness—there wasn't much more a person needed than that.

Well, companionship was always nice. As I dried my hair with a towel, I thought over how I would apologize to Del. And then I *had* to talk to him about other, weightier matters.

But first I had someone else to take care of. I came out of the bathroom and dressed quickly. No silk dresses for a while; it was a leggings-and-T-shirt kind of day.

"Here we go," I said to Midge once I was finally ready, booping her on the nose. Joanna was a dim, muddy amber on the walls as I walked to the door, her fractals twisting sluggishly—preoccupied with something, probably.

The door didn't open at my touch. I jabbed at the button again, thinking I hadn't pushed it hard enough.

Nothing.

"Joanna, the button—?"

The whoosh of the door opening, and the person just outside it, stayed my tongue. Midge gave a low growl, and I bent down to hold her back from doing anything worse.

"You're looking refreshed," Jexrah said, eyes glittering as she looked down at me. Today she'd opted for a dress constructed from fine, ruby red filaments that interlocked in an accordion fashion to billow about her body. The garment bounced and oscillated with the slightest movement, giving the impression that she'd wrapped herself in a couple dozen red Slinkies. I vaguely contemplated what happened when she sat down; did the fibers go all bent and matted beneath her, or did they spring back into shape when she got up?

"Had a good rest?" she asked.

"I did," I said. "A little longer than I'm used to. And you?" Thank God for retail instincts; I managed to keep a smile on my face even as anger rocked me. I'd set Joanna the task of maintaining a princess watch, so why hadn't she warned me? Especially after the khindrae had essentially drugged me for her own nefarious purposes.

"I'm doing quite well." Del's sister looked… electrified? You could just see the energy rolling off her, like she was on the verge of breaking into a song-and-dance number. I braced myself for the worst—perhaps video evidence of Del and me in each other's embrace, splayed in living color on the walls like a celebrity sex tape.

But instead Jexrah looked down at Midge, then back to me. "Oh, what perfect timing. I understand that you have to take them for outings. To defecate. Shall we?"

It was a real struggle to keep up the smile. I was probably looking more ventriloquist dummy than human. "You… want to walk my dog with me?"

"I do."

"Oh, what a nice suggestion!" I said brightly, wrangling what false sincerity I could manage. "But I'll have to decline. She gets a bit weird sometimes if strangers come along on her walks. Has a hard time deciding where to go." A straight-up lie—this unexpected visit had rocketed all my inner alarms to DEFCON 1. No way was I going to allow Midge anywhere near whatever was about to go down.

Jexrah cocked her head to the side, and her dress twitched, the sound of filament on filament like so many insect legs brushing softly against each other. "Very understandable," she said. "How about you and I take a walk together, though? I've something to discuss with you."

That last bit wasn't really a question that demanded an answer. What the khindrae wanted, the khindrae got; I could try to hold my own, but at the end of the day Jexrah was simply better than me at this political maneuvering. She'd been born into royalty, could probably throw down power moves in her sleep.

Hey, at least I had bigger boobs.

"Sure," I said, still chipper, and followed her down the hallway, leaving Midge in the room. Jexrah marched briskly before me; I felt rather like a wayward child, being marched to the principal's office by her teacher. The dress scintillated madly under the orb lights, its color echoed by Joanna's faint ghost, red now instead of amber. That might mean she was hard at work on something or worried. Or both. My dread deepened.

Jexrah brought us in the direction of the hothouse. Del was waiting at the entrance when we arrived, looking bored. He grazed me with the barest glance, then turned all his attention to his sister.

"Why have you gathered us?" he asked her, with a trace of steel in his voice.

"Patience, Delklor," she said. When she punched the button for the hothouse entrance, it slid open just fine. Joanna's red patterns roiled. "Let's all of us take a stroll."

The hothouse was as humid as ever. The warm, life-scented air normally put me in a good mood, but today it was oppressive, muggy. Sweat beaded on the back of my neck, and breathing felt uncomfortably close to sucking in water.

Jexrah strode down the white path, past the pool and the gazebo. Del walked beside me, and I wondered what he thought of the changes I'd made to the hothouse since I'd come here, for there were a lot of them. I'd skimmed away the pond scum; I'd used trellises to prop up those plants with heavier, drooping stalks; I'd pulled up any tuahdes I'd been able to locate, lest Midge brush them accidentally; I'd draped the hanging vines over the path atop higher boughs; I'd trimmed back much of the gnarled, dead undergrowth. We passed the spot where I'd planted my vegetables, now just a patch of dirt speckled with a few native volunteers—what would grow into dusty purple nitlahav plants, if my instincts were correct.

"You have done a lot of work here," he said neutrally.

"It keeps me occupied."

Del's sister came to a halt just before the path curved again and motioned for us to follow her into the foliage. "Indulge me," she said, when he opened his mouth in protest. With Jexrah in the lead, we picked our way forward. I'd spent hardly any time in this part of the hothouse yet; I'd looked it over once when I'd first gotten here and decided other areas required more work.

But Midge had spent time here, it soon became obvious. Though the way forward was choked with branches and vines, these were only obstacles for us taller bipeds. For a shorter, four-legged creature, the going looked relatively easy, and more than a few paw prints were pressed into the dark, loamy soil, as well as—I side-stepped quickly—a good amount of dog shit.

This was where Midge had been going—the place I'd been meaning to check for any remaining tuahdes.

The stink of feces rose as we ventured deeper, strengthened by the warm, thick air. But mixed with the stench emerged a distinct spicy scent that intensified with each step, swirling in hefty gusts all around us. The smell was utterly familiar, but I couldn't place it…

In front of me, Del stiffened and came to a halt. "Fascinating, isn't it?" Jexrah called back to us. I leaned to the right so I could see around him, and my mouth dropped open.

Like shining emeralds among the darker plants grew thick, bright vines of green. The vines had wrapped themselves around the lower halves of several tree trunks, like an anaconda squeezing its prey into the afterlife, and drooping off the ropy stalks were many bulging red fruits, each at least the size of a grapefruit: tomatoes, or a mutant version of them, along with their characteristic peppery scent. A whole bunch of them lay heaped on the ground, several bearing distinct bite marks, many of them sunken and wrinkled from rot. And I remembered that single, barely ripe tomato I'd given Midge to eat as a taste of home… a tomato with seeds that had passed through her into the hothouse's fertile ground to eagerly sprout and grow into this… monstrosity.

Jexrah turned to face us—or Del, rather. I was just the accessory to this conversation. "You see, I grew curious about all this time your guest has been spending in the hothouse. The ship steward reports that she has been amusing herself by conducting some quaint gardening experiments."

"Th-that's—" I started.

"She claims," she continued, still looking only at her brother, "that your guest has requested several different supplies and substances to coax local Earth plants to grow in our native dirt—all these experiments unfortunately bearing little success. *Soil issues*, I believe she said."

"I—"

"Well," she pressed on, gesturing to the distended fruits, "I see no issue. Which, if you can imagine, led me to be very interested in all these requests for various gardening chemicals. I asked your ship steward to run an analysis report detailing reasons why a person might request these materials, aside from gardening." Her eyes gleamed. "You'll never guess what she told me."

Beside me, Del was absolutely still. Dots swarmed in the corners of my vision.

"I'm sad to report that your guest has been trying to mix up homemade, low-level explosives. Gunpowder, I believe, is the human vocabulary term. I found traces of it in the gazebo this morning—oh, no need to worry, as I disposed of the materials with all the proper care."

I felt the full weight of Del's gaze swing toward me, but I couldn't look at him. "What is the meaning of this deception?" he asked me.

I said nothing—couldn't have said anything if I'd wanted to. Breathing was becoming difficult.

And Jexrah was radiating barely restrained delight. "My strong recommendation is immediate confinement to her quarters. I believe the ship steward has already taken several steps—"

"Leave us," Del told her in a low, measured voice.

"Delkl—"

"Leave us!" This a near roar. I flinched, shrinking back.

She did leave then, walking past us back toward the path sinuously, triumphantly. Just me and him now.

"Tell me why," he said after a few awful, furious seconds. "Were you thinking to kill me?"

That would be the first place his mind went, being royal. "I was going to try to use it to go home," I said in a small voice, still looking away. The heat of the air was doing nothing for me; my insides were cold, cold, cold. "I was going to try to blow a hole in the wall in the room downstairs—your old bedroom."

"You know of that room," he said, not really asking. All my

deceptions were being dragged out into the open, to stud the ground between us like upward-pointed knives.

"I—yes. I was going to blow a hole in the wall and steal an escape pod. But after we… the other night—" I broke off. "Doesn't matter."

I stole a glimpse at him and was sorry I had. The man I had spent the night with, who had sung me to sleep in his arms—gone. In that man's place was someone else entirely, looking at me like I was the stranger, and I suppose to him I was. My head swam.

"Of course you would try to leave," he said as if to himself. "You were required to stay here, given no other option. You're intelligent, resourceful. Brave. Of course you would."

"I need to sit down."

"You can do so back in your quarters."

"Del—"

"I should never have told you that name. A grave error on my part." Revoking any privileges he'd given me, as easily as he'd sent Joanna away. Something in his eyes had snapped shut, that darkness returning. At the sight of it, tears blurred my vision. I willed myself not to let them spill over in front of him.

"All right," I said, dazed. "All right." And I turned around and stumbled away from him.

Chapter Thirteen

I DON'T REMEMBER THE WALK BACK TO MY ROOM. PROBABLY Joanna moved alongside me, monitoring now with extra scrutiny this most dangerous of houseguests. Maybe Del followed at a distance, to make sure I made it back to the suite that would now serve as my much-smaller prison. I was just one moment in the hothouse and the next moment curled up on my bed, raw and wretched.

My heart had been wrenched around so much lately that there was nothing else for it but to cry, and so I did, for what felt like days. Every time the well of tears seemed close to drying up, I'd think of how he'd looked at me and start up again.

He hadn't even really seemed angry with me. More… resigned to see my human colors on full display at last. Del wasn't wrong; I'd had to try to leave, even though doing so had left me in fractured, sorry pieces.

And as the tears ran on, a soft realization: I didn't regret what I'd done.

At last I ran out of tears, though the awful, hollow feeling remained. I looked around the room, bleary-eyed and feeling tender. It felt wrong to be doing anything *but* crying.

The first thing I saw was that Midge, out of desperation, had relieved herself in the corner of the room near the mirror. "I'm sorry," I whispered to her, and she snuggled into my side, all forgiven and forgotten. If there's anything I know, it's that we don't deserve dogs.

I looked back at the mess in the corner, my mind starting to remember the realities of life again. Perhaps this would have to be our new normal, now that I was confined to my suite.

"Can a cleaner bot come take care of that please?" I asked the room softly. I would have done it myself, but I didn't have the right materials, and no way was Joanna going to fabricate any cleaning supplies for me now.

There was no reply, but Joanna had heard me; a few minutes later the door swooshed open to reveal the stocky form of a cleaner bot—and Meervit in drone form, hovering right above it.

"Hello," she said tinnily, gliding to a midair halt just before the foot of the bed. Midge's hackles rose, but I put an arm around her and she stayed put.

I wasn't happy to see the khindrae, and I certainly wasn't feeling up for any pleasantries. What I wanted to say was, *Were you trying to kill me the other night when you 'lost connection' with the pod?* It was starting to strike me as mightily convenient that Meervit had shared all her super-secret info with me so that I would in turn tell her all I knew (not much), only then to lose her connection and leave me floating in a precarious state. If the pod happened to crash headlong into the ground, killing the human on board—oh well. At least she'd found out if I was useful or not.

Yet, given my current tenuous situation, accusing the alien princess of half-hearted, attempted murder didn't seem overly bright. "Hello," I said, attempting a cordial tone.

"Your eyes…"

"It's from crying." Wouldn't it be nice for this drone, too, to become "unfortunately broken," so that I didn't have to have this conversation? I was about to lose it.

"Hm," Meervit said. "That's…"

"Tears. Moisture. From your eyes." I drew a breath, fed up and feeling bold. "Listen, the other night…"

"Oh!" she said, buzzing a little closer. "I really do owe you an apology for that. I'm sure it was a terrible fright for you, to be alone in the pod like that."

"It was."

Meervit made a sort of tutting sound. "The geomagnetic storm proved more intense than our model anticipated." Then she launched into an explanation about plasma and solar-wind streams and some other stuff that sailed right on over my head—very *doth the lady protest too much?*

My gut said, *she doth*, but Lord only knew the truth of it. From the corner, the cleaner bot gave a satisfied little trill, its job done, and trundled out of the room. "Whose idea was it to go star-gazing?" I asked as Meervit's science lecture wound to a close.

"My sister's."

"I'd thought there was going to be a set flight path…?" That's what Joanna had relayed to me.

"That was the original plan," she admitted, "but then my sister decided just a minute before you came in that she wanted to manually pilot her pod. And she mentioned there was a building geomagnetic storm, so I thought seeing the northern lights would be fun. Her steward sent me a report on the best viewing spot, and it seemed simple enough for me to wing us there manually. In any case, I'm sorry to have frightened you."

Jexrah, the heel—it was very convenient to blame her for everything, wasn't it? Even so, Meervit sounded sincere enough.

It's admittedly hard to judge a person's honesty when they're a small drone, though. Gah.

"Now," she said, "I really came by to discuss something else with you…"

I braced myself. "Go ahead." If there was anything I knew by now, it was that Del's sisters weren't the type to drop by for a casual chat.

"I wanted to discuss your future," she said, buzzing a little to the right, then to the left, like she was pacing before the bed. My future wasn't exactly looking bright at the moment. I motioned for her to continue.

"With today's… revelations," she said, "it's become quite obvious to me that your continued presence on board will prove difficult."

What in the world did *that* mean? A swift trip to Ailopt's version of prison?

I must have looked stricken. "Oh, I don't mean to frighten

you," she said quickly. "This is good news, not bad. Just a little while ago I flashed a message to the head of the Intelligent Alien Species Commission—just to apply a bit more pressure to expedite the original request for your release. As I understand it, the request has been a delicate thing to negotiate. None of this is strictly legal, of course.

"The commissioner did, fortunately, get back to me swiftly. As he tells me, it proved too difficult to delete your contact entry on the Intelligent Alien Species Registry entirely, given that the registry is under a great deal of outside scrutiny, with frequent audits. However, they were able to amend the entry to Ambassador status, despite any planned relationship with Earth being entirely too premature." She sighed. "And, in fact, the commissioner tells me that all of this was decided several days ago. His message must have gone astray when he flashed it to the ship. So my sincere apologies to you for the delay in communication."

She'd lost me ages ago. "I have no idea what you're talking about."

"Your contact entry on the Intelligent Alien Species Registry has been amended," she said a bit slower. "Your release has been granted."

"That means I don't have to go to prison?"

"No, Corinne," she said with the tone one used when speaking with someone unfortunately dim. "I'm talking about the Intelligent Alien Species Registry. I'm sure you're aware that you had a contact entry placed on the registry as soon as you came aboard?"

"Yes…?" That would be my dad's entry, which I had assumed during the electrical outage.

"Well, the status of your entry has been switched from Common to Ambassador. It means you can go home."

That couldn't be right. Surely I'd heard her wrong. "Go home?"

"To your family, yes."

"But—" I sputtered, trying to bring my mind to any sort of order. It was hard to think of anything with those four words drumming through my mind. *You can go home.* "You're saying this was all done days ago. The change to my, er, contact entry."

"Correct," said Meervit. "Again, the mix-up is most unfortunate, since you clearly wish so fervently to be back home. If it weren't for the delay in communication, I'm sure you wouldn't have felt pressed to take such… desperate measures. But with this good news, all that can stay in the past."

It was like I was trying to push my thoughts through molasses. None of this made sense. "But who requested the release?"

The nose of her drone dipped a little. I got the sense she was trying to see me more clearly, to judge if I really needed to know the answer or if I was just acting the fool. "The vrakhinahar made the request," she said slowly. "Shortly after you boarded the ship. You mean to say he never told you?"

My silence was answer enough. But in my mind, the words formed an incessant loop.

He never told you, he never told you, he never told you. Not about any of it, not even a hint. And whole days had passed since the final decision had been made.

Del hadn't told me he was trying to negotiate my release.

And a separate realization stabbed through me, with the searing burn of truth.

"He knew," I said hollowly. In my chest, whatever still remained after all the tears was sinking, shriveling. "He never told me about requesting a release, and he never told me when the release was granted. But he knew." And it had been days. Days when I could have been home with my dad, let him know I was all right, wasn't dead. A lie by omission was still a lie, and Del had *lied*.

The drone came closer, and I drew back. "Corinne, listen to me very carefully," Meervit said. Her voice had shifted to a lower, harder register, and for the first time I saw clear as day how similar she was to her sister. "What I am telling you is that there was an unanticipated delay in the communication on the part of the commissioner. Please do not make me repeat myself. The vra-khinahar acted charitably to you by negotiating for your contact entry to be amended to Ambassador status, and *that is it*. You should ready yourself to leave."

She knew there was something between Del and me. She might not know about the other night, but she'd guessed the rest of it well enough. "Ambassador status—what does that mean?" I asked, grasping for whatever information I could get.

Her voice grew colder still, and I shivered. "It doesn't matter. What does matter is that you get to leave now. Do you understand me? You are leaving."

And I would not be coming back.

Once she left, I got off the bed, stood in the middle of the room. I was quivering with… rage? Sorrow? And not a bit of it felt real.

He couldn't really have kept that from me—could he?

I'd slept with him. The thought thudded through me, knocking the air out of my lungs. Had he known then? Had he kept me here, slept with me, knowing all the while I was free to leave?

"I need to talk to him." My voice didn't sound like my own. Rougher. Older. I floated outside myself a little.

The silence afterwards was lengthy—lengthy enough that I wondered if the added security features didn't permit Joanna to talk to me or if this was her giving me the cold shoulder.

At last: "He doesn't wish to speak with you."

"You tell him exactly what Meervit just told me, then ask again." Midge looked at me and gave a soft, high whine.

"He—"

"Tell him," I said, my voice strained, "that the woman he slept with would like to know the exact moment he decided to become my jailer. Surely His Royal Highness is courageous enough to answer one simple question."

Then I waited. Time stretched long, and I began to suspect he wasn't coming (and also began to think about what that meant in answer to my question). I started feeling like I was going to throw up, and I sat down in the blue armchair, laid my head back and closed my eyes, took a few deep breaths.

They did little to steady me.

The door opened with a pneumatic hiss. I gritted my teeth and opened my eyes.

"The commissioner flashed the message to me the day after," Del said solemnly. "In the evening."

He stood opposite me. There was a tautness in his face, but I wasn't looking at him, not really; I was too busy running over his words in my mind, trying to hear if they rang true or stank of a lie. It was hard to know anything for certain with so many thoughts and hopes and fears churning through me.

"And when did you first ask the commissioner if I could be taken off the registry?" I asked.

"Within a day of your boarding," he said quietly. "After the panic attack. It was clear to me that you should be allowed to go home, damn the registry."

"And you never thought to tell me."

"Of course I thought to tell you," he said, sounding strangled. "I *agonized* over when would be the best time to tell you, and then I convinced myself that the real question was whether I *should* even tell you at all. It was a question of… giving you false hope. I am afforded many things, being who I am, but there was never any guarantee… And then…" His stony voice trailed off, lips trembling, and I wasn't so obtuse that I couldn't hear his thoughts through the silence. *And then things happened between us. A strange acquaintanceship that became a friendship. Signals back and forth. The kiss.*

So that had been the first falsehood, which stung but was understandable, and perhaps forgivable. The second lie, though… "Then," I said, "the commissioner told you my contact entry had been changed. To Ambassador status, whatever that means."

"Yes," he admitted. "He flashed the message to us the evening after that night." After the night we'd spent together was what he meant. "If you'd like," he said, "I can show you the ship's communication log. It would have the time."

"No," I said, shaking my head; Joanna could fake whatever proof he needed. But I found that I believed him, because small things were coming to mind now, all of them after our night together: his absence, and the odd way he'd looked at me during the dinner party. How he'd cringed away from me afterwards, when he'd brought me back to my suite. There had been the change in Joanna's mood, too, several days ago, her strange, preoccupied sullenness. And then whatever conversation I'd overhead the two of them having in Ziryahshun, when I'd been near out of my mind from the maht.

They'd been discussing me, and what to do about me. No way to know that for certain, of course, but I could feel it in my bones, with the sharp, ringing clarity of a bell.

Del wasn't meeting my eyes, because the next thing I said would so obviously be the jackpot question. "And when were you going to tell me I could leave?" I asked, finally. I was finding that I didn't really know what to do with my hands, whether I should clasp them or wring them or keep them clenched to my sides. Punching something—someone—might have felt really good. "How long did you plan on keeping me here? Was there a—a plan? Another day? Another week, or a month? Get me to Tenctah, then let me know?" I swallowed. "Get me more… *invested* first?"

"No," he said, looking appalled. "No. I had no plan. And I thought of it constantly, how happy you would be if—when—I told you. You've wanted so badly to go home, any person could see… No, I could never have brought you to Tenctah, under the circumstances. But I did wait to tell you," he said hoarsely. "I was selfish. And"—I could see written plainly on his face how much the next words pained him to say aloud—"I was afraid."

"Afraid," I repeated, narrowing my eyes. A livid heat was smoldering beneath my skin, goading me to scream.

"That you would leave. Afraid that—that you would not consider staying." His eyes held mine as he said it, and cold shivers danced over me.

"I'd thought about it," I said distantly, feeling more and more sick. My head was ringing. Surely this was all just a terrible dream. I'd wake up soon from this latest maht-fueled nightmare to him holding my hand, pressing a kiss to my cheek.

"You'd thought to stay," he said, and something in his face shifted. I hated how I could look at him and still see the person I'd come to know. I wanted to see him as a stranger, an alien once more, because I couldn't reconcile him keeping these things from me. That was the sort of thing a stranger would do, someone callous, hard-hearted—not *him*, of all people.

"Forget it. That's all done," I said, in the way that you tell yourself a new reality to affirm it. Whoever that person was that

I'd considered staying for—that person didn't exist. There was nothing for me here but lies heaped on lies.

"Corinne—"

"Stop," I said, shaking my head. "Please stop. It was all over anyway, with the gunpowder." He'd said so himself, though not in so many words.

"But…" He blinked, confusion lancing through his expression. I'm sure I looked just as strange to him right now as he did to me, with all our truths pulled out into the light.

"I want to go home now."

"I understand," he said softly, though his eyes pled with me, with a quiet, private desperation. "Of course. You'll want time to pack. Afterwards Joanna can inform—"

"No. I want to go home *now*." I didn't know any other way to say it. "No packing—I don't want a thing from you." I still had my winter things from the day I'd been abducted, shoved into the back of the armoire behind all my fabricated frippery. Besides, it felt good to be cruel. "A few minutes is all I need, then we can leave."

His eyes glittered strangely at me, and I remembered again how rumae didn't possess the anatomy to cry. A crazed part of me wondered what he would look like right now if he did.

He bowed his head. "A few minutes, then. I'll be just outside."

I nodded. And when he turned to walk away, I closed my eyes and didn't watch him go.

Chapter Fourteen

IT WAS ONLY THE WORK OF A MINUTE OR TWO TO PULL OUT MY winter gear and put my hair back into a ponytail. I wasn't sure how this next part would go, but it was safe to say there was a walk in the woods ahead of me.

As I shrugged on my coat, I felt the weight of my phone hanging in the pocket. I'd left it in there, since it had been a useless brick ever since it had died in the snowstorm. I reached in, skimming a finger over the mirrored smoothness of the dark screen, and felt a stirring of warmth in my chest. Soon, maybe even within the hour, I would be back in the world of human things: cars, phones, TVs, all the miscellany of modern life. There would be plants that were green, magic-less mirrors, furniture sized to fit me, and, most importantly, human beings themselves.

Midge's tail wagged slowly when I knelt to strap her into her bottle-green coat and dog booties. The scent of home must have still been clinging to her clothes; I was sure she had some inkling about what was happening.

"Ready?" I asked her, and her hind end wiggled faster. Oh yes, she knew.

The last thing I did before I left the room was to tuck my sketchbook into one of the coat's inner pockets, to be my one memento of my time here. Of course there were other hidden mementoes, carved into me. I was different now from the person I'd been prior to the abduction. But this would be the one tangible thing I'd bring back with me.

"Goodbye, Joanna," I said to the melancholy, dusty gray ghost in the corners of the room. The gray shivered, rippled a little.

"Goodbye, Corinne."

I gave a little nod to her, before casting a last glance around the room.

Then I left.

Del was waiting for me right outside, just like he'd said he would. I looked at him, and he looked at me, and then he didn't say anything at all, just turned and led me down the hallway. Midge was a dark presence at my side, near underfoot in her quiet excitement.

It was a grim, silent walk to the exit-portal room, which was right next door to the entrance-portal room, as it turned out. Both rooms had naturally been off-limits throughout my time here, but now we strode straight in. The exit-portal room was small, square, and devoid of any furniture.

I looked up; there was that same complicated, garbage-chute-looking hole that had deposited me onto the *Huivnarrut*, its interior mechanism faintly gleaming through the shadows.

"We're going up that?" I asked.

"Yes. You should hold onto her," he said, motioning to Midge.

"You're coming with us?"

"Of course." His tone brooked no discussion. I hoisted Midge into my arms, then gave him a sharp nod. I was still reeling; it hurt to look at him.

Del gave a terse command in Ziryahshun. The walls, blank gray before, lit up red. Above us, the chute clicked as its machinery engaged and folded back. Deep in the center of the hole, I caught a brief glimpse of shimmering, beautiful darkness—that same mysterious force that had siphoned us up onto the ship so long ago.

I thought of the brief journey through space Del had taken me on when he'd shown me Tenctah, all those stars around us like pinholes to another world.

With a rush of air, the portal drew me upward, my feet peeling off the floor. I held onto Midge for all it was worth as she shook in my arms. The blackness swirled around us, and I coughed; I'd forgotten the battering air pressure of this shadow space.

But soon enough we were through, leaving the darkness for brilliant sunlight. It was early in the day still, about eleven a.m. if I had to guess. Floating in midair, I chanced a look downward. As before, the snow below had been molded into swooping geometric designs—some consequence of the ship's hovering presence, I understood now. I raised my gaze. Today was gorgeous as a painting: gray mountains, white snow, blue sky.

We floated gently downward, our descent much smoother than the ascent had been. Whatever technological magic made this possible was causing the open air to be thick and soupy and strange.

And then we touched down, and with a muted pop the air went back to normal. Midge was barking like mad, and I let her slip from my arms as I sucked in a breath of real, frigid air. The cold needled the inside of my lungs. I'd forgotten what that felt like.

There was a creaking of snow from behind me, and I turned towards Del. It was odd to see him out of the context of the ship, in my world. He hadn't donned any cold-weather gear—rumae machismo at work?—and I wondered if he was cold, then told myself to stop caring.

I looked up to give myself a last look at the ship, but it wasn't there—not the swirling black hole, nor the dimpled, silver-green metal of the actual ship. Just bright, cloudless sky. Of course, that was a cloaking projection.

So I'd seen the last of the *Huivnarrut*.

"I'm going now," I said, unsure of what else to say now that the moment had arrived. The words *I'll miss you* sprang to mind—but no, not after what he'd done.

"Yes," he said simply.

So, numb, I started walking forward. The crunch of footsteps in snow followed me, and emotion came back to me then, in a sharp burst of anger. "What are you doing?"

"I'm walking with you," he said.

"You don't need to do that. I don't *want* you to do that."

He looked at me evenly. "Are there not wild beasts here, in these mountains?"

"Well, yes."

"I'm walking with you." He scanned our surroundings. "Joanna has told me that that the way back lies in that direction."

I'd made a rough guess as to the way home based on where the sun hung in the sky. The direction Del was pointing was about ten degrees off from that. Perhaps fifteen degrees.

"That's where I was going," I said. He was wise enough not to answer me.

We walked on. Thankfully, the sounds of the forest were there to fill the silence between us. Birds called, tree trunks creaked. Once or twice I heard the soft plop of snow as it dropped from a tree branch to the ground below. I found I was waiting for Earth's nature to fill me up, to buoy my spirits and distract from the day's awfulness.

But I was empty.

It didn't take long to arrive at the meadow. Its white was crusted over with a thin layer of ice, so that it gleamed like glass. And, beyond that, our farmhouse. Christmas Eve—we always made sure to have lights up, but I couldn't see any at all. Midge panted as she paced the edge of the meadow, eager to cross; she was keeping me in her peripheral vision, waiting for my signal. I couldn't see the driveway from this angle, couldn't see if my dad's truck was parked, but I had a sixth-sense feeling he was home.

Time hung still.

"You should go," Del said from beside me. His words were

soft, like the low rumble of far-off thunder.

"I—"

"Corinne," he said firmly. "Go." Then, in a rockier tone: "I will… be glad. To know that you're happy."

I gave him a sharp little nod. A second or two trickled by. A few more—sand in an hourglass. Oh, I hadn't thought, even after all the lies, that I would feel ripped in two like this.

But still I went, springing forward with an animal instinct towards the meadow. Every footstep crackled beneath me as my boots punched through the ice. Ahead of me, Midge beat a swift course forward, like a dark arrow against the white of the snow.

Of course she reached the back door first, and she scrabbled at the handle with her claws, making an awful whining noise I'd never heard from her before. The door opened, and my dad was there, looking down at Midge, then up at me. I'd never seen him more shocked, like two ghosts had appeared on his doorstep.

"You—" he started, and I'd made it to the door now, falling into his arms. He brought me in for a hug, and the both of us started crying right there in the doorway, with Midge leaping all around us.

After a minute more of hugging and crying and blubbering, my dad put his arm around me and made to bring me inside. I could tell he didn't want to let go of me, like the slightest breeze might waft me away. And I realized that, somehow, I felt like that had already happened. I wasn't all there, it seemed… some part of me still back on the ship.

Just before the door closed, I turned my head to look across the meadow. No one there. He had gone, and it was really all over. For the first time in however long, everything in sight was from my planet.

Why couldn't that sit right with me?

THE PROBLEM WAS THAT SHE WASN'T THE KIND OF GIRL YOU COULD easily forget. Other girls he'd been with were disposable, really just a novelty to play with. A few words, followed by a half-hearted pursuit, and his looks took care of the rest—they spilled the secrets of their bodies to him easily and eagerly. Flesh splayed open over the sheets—it was sadly anticlimactic, though he did always manage to finish.

Yet she had asked for more from him. She hadn't made it easy, and the challenge of it had worked its way inside him and lodged deep, like a tapeworm. And during the chase came the heady realization that she was the type of girl you made a wife out of. A mother.

So he'd gone through all the proper motions, and when those hadn't worked, well, it was time to up the ante. He loved her, right? Surely this was love? So the next step was to declare it and force some action from her.

He'd been certain it would work.

But it hadn't, and she'd disgraced him there on the road, before all those people. Oh, the town's gossip mill had moved on to other things, and the front of the truck was fixed and good as new, but the wound from his humiliation remained, open and smarting. And the worm hungered.

Then he'd heard she'd gone to Texas. Texas! Without telling a soul save for her dad, like a runaway fleeing in the night. They said she wanted to get away from it all. Take a break.

At first he'd thought her departure would provide a balm for the worm. Maybe even a cure. But it proved to be just the opposite, for the more he thought about it, her leaving like that meant she was just as affected as he was. And that tidbit of knowledge was more than enough to feed the worm.

So it grew, eating him from the inside. He could always feel it, twitching, squirming around, or taut as a bow string when he thought of her and touched himself.

Nothing helped; the worm continued its torment. He thought about heading to Texas to track her down. One night he idled in the truck in the driveway for a long, unmeasured time, wondering if he might just go right then and there. The thought of what he'd do once he found her brought him to the brink—so much tantalizing possibility. It was almost enough to drive him mad.

But he held out against the instinct. She'd be back; that's what everyone else said, and he had the sense they were right. So he would wait it out, being consumed in the meantime. No matter; he'd almost learned to like the feeling of the worm gnawing away at him. Waiting would just make her return all the more sweet.

Chapter Fifteen

"HE LET YOU GO," MY DAD SAID, ONCE HE'D SITUATED ME AT OUR dinette table. In front of me was a giant mug of black coffee, a plate of shortbread cookies from someone's wife at work, half a carton of potato salad from Robinsons, a grilled cheese sandwich my dad had been about to eat himself, our once-a-year fruitcake special-ordered by my aunt in Texas, and a tin of dollar-store-looking candy canes.

"They fed me, you know," I said.

"Huh." He looked unconvinced. "Regular food?"

"No, not really." He gave me an insistent look, and I obligingly took a bite of potato salad. It was great.

"He let you go," my dad repeated.

"Yes."

"No… catches?" *What had I given up to come back here?* was what he really meant—a father's worry for his abducted daughter spilling in infinite, nightmarish directions.

"No," I said, looking about our dinette. The dusty cuckoo clock on the wall that hadn't cuckooed for years and years…

the tiny CRT kitchen TV… the faint pencil marks to the right of the fridge, where I'd stood tall every new school year to be measured… I looked at all these things, remembering. Had the kitchen always been so small? Had our table always been just this shade of shellacked walnut brown?

I'd heard the story of my Polish great-great-great-granddad so many times, had a sort of oral-history film reel in my mind of his story—how he'd gone west, struck gold, married the young widow, settled our land, et cetera, et cetera… but no one had mentioned if, after all that, he'd ever gotten the chance to return to Poland. Or even if he'd ever visited the East Coast again.

Probably not, in those times. But I found myself wondering how he would have felt to do so.

"And you're all right?" my dad said.

"I'm all right." *I don't know* was what I really meant.

I mustered a smile—really gave it my all. "I'm all right," I said again, reaching across the table to touch his hand.

"Okay," my dad said slowly. His eyes, still watery, weren't leaving me, not even for a second. That brought another ball of tears to my throat, and I looked down at the plate of cookies, concentrating on that. The cookies blurred, and it took choking a few of them down before I was good to talk again.

Talk we did, in bits and pieces and many generalities. Discussing the last few weeks in broad strokes suited me just fine, and I got the sense that, actually, my dad didn't care much about what had happened.

Just as long as I was home.

And of course I didn't give even the smallest hint about anything that had occurred between Del and me. My dad would think it awful. Monstrous. My abduction had caused him enough worry, and I didn't want to add on any more.

That conviction was redoubled when I stood up to go to the bathroom and caught sight of the living-room wall behind me.

Normally we did up the living room really nice with Christmas decorations, but not this year. Instead, in the corner where the tree should be, my dad had pulled all our family pictures from the wall and taped up many, *many* sheets of A4 paper. They hung limply like strange, textured wallpaper, overlapping here and there, and they were printed with… I was too far away to see. So I wandered closer, slack-jawed, and saw they were what could best be described as lunatic articles about aliens, all clearly straight from our ancient inkjet printer. The only thing missing was a web of red thread and pushpins to tie everything together.

"Research," my dad said when I looked back at him with raised eyebrows.

"Uncle Ed's Forum of the Weird, Secret, and Inexplicable?" I read wonderingly from one sheet.

His cheeks turned a bit pink. "They were one of the better sources, actually."

"Dad."

"Well, I didn't know what to *do*, Corinne! What was I supposed to do? People would find out eventually that something had happened to you. And I couldn't tell them my daughter had been abducted by aliens. They'd've thought I was crazy—

you know they would have." I thought about it. Yes, they would have. "And then maybe they'd think... well, that I'd done something to you."

"So what *did* you tell them?" I asked, dazed.

"I told anyone who needed to know that you were really beaten up about the breakup and wanted to get out of town for a bit." The breakup. Joe. I kept almost forgetting about that. It felt like that had been years—light-years—ago.

"Get out of town... to where?"

"I said you'd gone to visit Aunt Misty in Houston," he said. "That was just to buy me time. Not the greatest lie, but— Anyway, then I took time off work. Used all my days."

"You used all your days for this?" I asked, motioning to the lunatic articles. *Do the Greys Have Ears?* read one. *What the Government Isn't Telling Us About the Pleiades!!!* clamored another.

"Yes, some of it." He huffed at the articles. "Not a one of these was useful. Mostly I was out there looking for you. I found the clearing with the strange snow, of course, but there wasn't anything besides that left to see. No spaceship, nothing. I took some potshots at the sky a few times, just to try."

"I was up there," I said. "They have this technology... You can't see the ship."

"I hoped that was the case. But I thought maybe they'd taken you back to wherever they were from. I thought that... maybe—" He looked away, voice wobbly.

"But it wasn't that way, Dad," I said carefully, giving him a side-hug as I led him back to the kitchen table. We were both of us supporting the other right now.

We ate some more cookies, and we each had a little slice of fruitcake. It was gluey and delicious. I got up to make another pot of coffee and marveled again at how everything in the kitchen felt just the littlest bit off. Give Goldilocks enough time, and she'll get used to the three bears' home.

"So what about my job?" I asked when I joined him at the table again. "I hope you talked to Ray?"

"I did," he said. "Well, he was pretty puzzled about you taking off like that, but he said of everyone working there you were the one most deserving a break."

"A break…?" I squinted. "So does that mean I still have a job?"

"You'll have to talk to Ray, of course. I'm sure he wasn't too pleased that you were just gone all of a sudden. But I think, the way he was talking… could be?"

Well, that gave me something to take care of, and I was happy for it. Anything to keep my mind on things mundane and ordinary.

My phone was still bricked, and I knew it would have a million texts from Molly when I did turn it on, so I left it off and charging, then made the call from our house phone.

Everyone freaked out, which seemed like an overkill response to the story my dad had told Ray. I mean, on the surface of it, I was a retail worker who'd left her low-wage job to sojourn in Texas—not too crazy of a story. But I guess for anyone who knew me, my actions had seemed like a big deal. "I was sure you'd had a mental breakdown," Molly told me, once she'd hightailed it over to our house. "To not text me at all? I mean… *did* you have a mental breakdown?"

"No," I said, looking out the window, across the snowy meadow. "Well, sort of, I suppose."

"I didn't even think you liked your Aunt Misty that much."

"She's okay, if you don't mind all the talk about ghosts and angels. Do you think Ray will take me back?" We hadn't gotten that far on the phone; I'd just called to say I was home and then Ray had yelled out the news to everyone and they'd passed the phone around and Molly had said she'd be right over and hung up.

"He'd better," she said, "or he'll have a mutiny on his hands. Lord, we've missed you." She peered at me as I nibbled another cookie. "You seem different."

"Probably I'm tanner. The weather was nice."

"Hm, you don't look that tan. You're sure you're feeling better?"

"I'm fine, Mol. Happy to be home."

She looked at me a second or two longer, considering, before reaching for the candy-cane tin. "Well, I'm glad you're back. You meet any cute cowboys down there? Joe's been freaking out."

I clutched at the lifeline of her last sentence, so I could avoid the one before it. "Really? How so?"

She ripped the cellophane off a candy cane, popped it in her mouth, then took it right on out again. "These are stale. Um, it's hard to say what's really going on with him. Just... you can see he's not himself. Worried about you, I'm sure. I keep seeing him over at Arlene's, brooding. You'd better be prepared—I'm sure he'll come over here once he hears you're back."

No doubt he already knew; word gets around fast in small towns.

"You're sure you're not seeing someone?" she continued, looking at me closely again. "You seem a little... I don't know. Lovelorn."

I couldn't help it; I hesitated. "Oh my God," she said, sitting up straight. "Oh my God, you—"

I motioned for her to keep her voice down. My dad was off somewhere else in the house, giving us some girl time, but I'd noticed that he kept wandering through the kitchen for this or that.

She leaned forward, eyes agleam. "Okay, secret romance."

"We broke up, Mol," I said in a small voice.

"But... you don't look like you did when you broke up with Joe. This is different. You're not happy about it. You guys had a fling, then you figured you had to come home, and he didn't want to do long distance, so he broke up with you, and— Oh, he might be in Houston, but I'm still going to kill him."

"He didn't break up with me," I admitted. I couldn't believe she'd teased this out of me so quickly. "It was... mutual? We'd kept things from each other." Understatement of the year.

"What things?" Then she saw my face and waved her hands. "Never mind, forget I asked." Molly's nosy about my love life, but above that she's a good friend. "Well, what's he like? What's his name?"

"Uh, Dale." Close enough. "He's... caring. Intelligent. I like talking with him."

"Hot?"

I shifted in my chair. "He's my type."

"Tall, dark, and handsome—got it. What else?"

"He... has a real sense of duty. He's honorable." Or was he? I was still struggling to square the events of this morning with the person I'd thought Del to be.

Molly picked up on the same incongruity. "But this honorable man lied to you."

"Yes..."

"Cheating?"

"No!"

"Okay then. And you'd lied to him, too."

I picked at a hangnail. "It was a difficult situation."

"Hm. Did you meet his family at all? How're they?"

"Er, not necessarily welcoming. It's a pretty close family. They see me as an outsider."

"Italian?" she guessed, then laughed at the face I made. "Okay, so to recap: he's a great guy, but there's the whole long-distance thing, plus his family's judgy. Plus he lied to you. But also you lied to him. Were they both kind of big lies?" she asked, and I bit my lip as I nodded. "Well," she continued, sighing, "it's not *good* to be lying to each other, obviously. But the way I see it, you tell a big lie, he tells a big lie..." She waggled her head back and forth. "Now, I don't know the details—and this *really* depends on the situation, but just hear me out... Couldn't you say those two lies kind of cancel each other out?"

I looked down at the plate of shortbread cookies, which unfortunately held only crumbs. "I don't know," I said slowly. "I can't really tell how I feel about it."

"You only found out recently about the lie, I'm going to guess? Yes? Then I'd say give it time."

"Oh, it's over," I said. "I'm here, he's… in Houston. It has to be over."

She gave me a little smile. "But that wasn't why you said you broke up. The distance wasn't the issue, it was whatever he didn't tell you."

"But—" As I was leaned forward to protest I felt the quick slither of metal around my neck as my necklace chain slid free from my shirt.

"Oh, Corinne!" Molly's eyes had gone wide. "Did he give you *that?*" In my haste to leave I'd forgotten all about the morganite necklace Joanna had fabricated for me that first day on the ship.

"No—er…"

"Oh, come on, he did! He must have! You're not telling me your Aunt Misty gave that to you."

"Well, no." Damn Molly and her psychic abilities.

"It's gorgeous. That's real?"

"It's…"

"What kind of stone is it?"

"Morganite, I think."

She leaned in close and caught the fine chain between her fingers, then turned the jewel this way and that. Then she gave me an appraising look.

"So he's a rich, thoughtful, hot, caring cowboy. I fail to see the problem besides the fact that the both of you had a little misunderstanding and that you'll probably move away to Texas."

"But it was more than a little misunderstanding."

"And you can't just tell me—? No, you won't. Okay. Well, all I'm asking is for you to just not write him off completely in your mind yet. Give it time." I started to protest, but she shushed me. "If there's anything I've learned being married to Kurt, it's that people are human." Well... "They're going to make mistakes. And I've just never seen you like this, Corinne! Definitely not with Joe, poor guy. So that's all I'll say! Just give yourself more time to think things through."

It was decent advice, I guess, for a woman with a beau living in Houston. But Del could be who knows where at this point, and I had no way to contact him.

And didn't want to contact him, more importantly. The knowledge of what he'd kept from me still smarted. So I smiled a little and nodded and made noises so that Molly would leave satisfied that I'd taken her advice to heart.

But what I really did was pack her advice into a little box in the back of my mind, hoping I'd forget she had gifted it to me. She didn't know the real situation, would have had a different opinion if she knew all the details.

Ray called me later that day to discuss coming back to the shop after Christmas. He was going to put one of the college kids on a later shift so I could work in the mornings; he knew I liked that. People might treat me with kid gloves for a while, I realized, since it was apparently understood that I'd had a mental breakdown.

Yes, please, I told Ray as my dad snuck glances at me from the other room. *Yes, I'd love to come back. I've missed everyone so much.*

It seemed I would be able to slip back into the familiar folds of my former life.

I had a hard time sleeping that night. My bedroom was exactly as it had always been: small, a bit dusty, everything exactly where I'd left it, and that was somehow just as odd as my dad's wall of (now removed) alien research. There were my slippers, there was my purse, there was my stack of borrowed paperbacks, now overdue. My eyes were automatically drawn to the walls, but they were still and ordinary, covered in the tea-rose-patterned wallpaper I'd had since childhood.

You could almost think the last few weeks had been nothing more than a dream.

Christmas was a quiet day for us. Thankfully I'd done my shopping early, so I had a nice leather wallet to give my dad. He'd gotten me a shiny new trowel and a sun hat, and he gave them to me a bit weepy-eyed. Naturally, he hadn't thought I would be here for Christmas—had wondered if I was dead.

We watched Christmas movies the rest of the day, then ate a simple dinner of green beans, steaks, and mashed potatoes. I attempted an apple tart, which came out all right, especially with a bunch of whipped cream over top. We didn't talk about what had happened out in the woods. Once or twice during the day I made movements to indicate I was going to take Midge for a walk, and my dad stopped me each time. "I'll take her—you rest here."

It was understandable; this ordeal had left scars on both of us.

The next day I went to work.

I think there would have been more of a hullabaloo if it

weren't for people thinking I was in a delicate state. As it was, everyone sort of gathered round when I came in, asking in their own sensitive way if I'd had a nice time off. Ray's wife had baked a cake—*Welcome Back!* on top in red, gloopy icing—which was excellent.

"Tell her thanks from me," I said to Ray, then asked if we could step into his office to have a quick chat about whatever had changed around the shop since I'd been gone.

"Oh, it's the same old place, Corinne," he said, shaking his head. "Nothing really changes here—you know that."

And just like my house, I found that to be the case.

But I had changed. Everyone said so, or if they didn't say so explicitly, they did whenever they looked at me, their gaze lingering maybe a second or two longer than necessary. *You seem different*, many people said, though no one could agree on the reason why. Was I tired? Was I standing up a little straighter, maybe, or was I slouching, or had I lost weight? Was something on my mind, or perhaps was I angry? A few customers asked if I'd just moved here from somewhere else. An older woman took one look at me and said, in a low, knowing voice, "There, there—it will all get better soon."

As I'd predicted, some alien quality had rubbed off on me.

In a midnight panic a few nights later, I rushed to the twenty-four-hour Walmart in Scarlettville to buy a pregnancy test. It came back negative, which I'd known it would—but had had to check. Rumae and humans might have their similarities, but I couldn't imagine the genetics lined up enough to allow for conception. I had the sense, too, that I would have been able to *feel* if I was pregnant, and (physically) I felt my usual self.

A few more days passed, and Dad made me book a physical, even though I'd had my annual visit only two months ago. "Just to make sure all that alien food didn't mess you up somehow." Wincing a little, I let Ray know that I had a doctor's appointment scheduled and would need to come in late that day—I didn't like having to ask for time off so soon after I'd come back—and he told me, in a serious sort of voice, that it sounded like a good idea for me to get checked out.

"Oh, I'm fine," I told him. "Really."

"Of course you are," he said, and I felt his gaze stay on me as I left the back office.

The matter of Joe had been simmering on the back burner, and the Sunday after I got back—my day off—our doorbell rang around one o'clock, and, well, there he was, back burner no longer. My dad had rushed to answer the door (more protectiveness, like he feared Del would wait patiently on our stoop for me to open the door, only to whisk me away again).

"Corinne," I heard Dad say. "You… have a caller."

It was sadly too cold to have whatever this conversation was to be out on our front step; I had to invite him in. Which I did, offering him a seat at our kitchen table, then a glass of water. None of this I did smilingly—just out of a host's necessary duties. As I brought two glasses of water back to the table, it struck me that this was a strange sort of thing for Joe to do, showing

up at his ex-girlfriend's house unannounced, when I, by all accounts, had suffered some serious mental distress on account
of our recent split.

"I'm glad you're back," he said once I sat down. He squinted
at me. "You look different."

"I caught a bit of a tan in Texas."

"You don't look tan. You look... I don't know. Something else."

"Funny lighting in this room," I said, nodding toward the
picture window, where I found my gaze often straying as of
late. "Why are you here, Joe?"

He reached for his water glass, but didn't take a sip, gathering his words, and I used the moment to study him. If I didn't
seem myself, like everyone insisted on telling me, then Joe was
right there, too. His dark hair, normally coiffed with gel, hung
lank, and his eyes were too bright. It was uncomfortable to look
at him; you could just see the tension seething through him.

"I know," he started, "that you... needed your time away."
His grip was too tight around his glass. "I've been using this
time, too, to think about where we went wrong. We should
start over, Corinne. I want you to— Please, let me *show* you the
man I can be for you. For us."

"Joe," I said, as gently as I could manage through my anger.
"There is no 'us.'"

His thumb was rubbing the top of his glass, worrying at it.
There had to be a groove in the rim, some little crack. "Now, I
gave you that space you needed," he said. "No questions asked.
Remember that. And now you're back—it's been a couple

days, and I gave you those, too. But it's time we had this conversation…"

He was still talking, but I wasn't hearing him. Something wasn't right here, and a few words started to murmur in my mind. *Delusional. Fixated.* And here, at my own kitchen table, that unsettling, sliding sensation reared again, the same feeling I'd had with him in the car just before we'd hit the deer, where I'd silently reached for my phone.

I wouldn't stand to feel that way in my own house.

"Are you listening to me?" he asked, grasping the glass tighter. The tips of his fingers were white.

"Joe. We're not together. Now, I'm sorry, but I'm going to have to ask you to leave."

He stared at me for a silent moment, and it was a look from a person I'd never met before, like some other being was peering out at me from beneath Joe's skin. Or perhaps this was the real Joe, laid bare, all the layers of charm and charisma and good looks stripped away.

A muscle in his jaw clenched. *He might hit me*, I thought.

And I did something I would later come to analyze and pick over and, sometimes, regret. "Dad," I called, and he was there a moment later.

It took only a second for him to feel the mood in the room and know that I wanted Joe gone. "Time to get going, son," he said and moved to hustle Joe out of the house. I don't know exactly what was said on the porch between the two of them, but I can well imagine it. *You'll leave my daughter alone from now on, or I'll make you wish you had.* Something to that effect.

Inside, I was still seated at our kitchen table, looking down at my hands, at the two glasses of water, then out the big picture window again. The whole scene just now had thrust me into a shivery, shaky state. How nice it would be if—someone—was here right now, to hold me, to rub warmth and comfort back into me.

But no, I couldn't think like that. He'd betrayed me, and he was gone.

Now, later on, I've thought over those few minutes Joe spent in our house more times than I'd care to admit. Of course, I didn't want the tension between us to spill over and get physical. But the male ego is a complex thing, and I've given a lot of thought to the way Joe left our house that day. If I'd spoken with him a while longer, handled matters myself, or given one of his friends or his parents a call after he'd gone… I still do catch myself wondering if those things might have prevented what happened afterward between Joe Gagnon and me.

Chapter Sixteen

December gave way to a merciless, frigid January. I went to the doctor, who prodded and palpated me, listened to my heart and lungs, took blood, had me pee in a cup to check once more if I were pregnant...

All tests pointed to me being a hearty, healthy, non-pregnant woman. "But have you considered talking with someone?" she asked me, when the exam was finishing up. "You don't seem yourself, if you don't mind my saying so." And she handed me a card for a therapist in town she recommended.

I smiled at her, took the card, and slipped it into my bag, to mingle with all the other bottom-feeder purse detritus, never to be seen or heard from again.

Despite the weather, I took to going on long walks after work, in whatever direction my feet wanted to take me—though not to *that* part of the woods. My dad wasn't necessarily happy about this development, but what was he going to do about it? Both he and I knew I wasn't the sort who could just be at work, be at home, be at work, be at home—I'm not made for the shut-in life. And for a gardener, too, winters are hard, since all you have are houseplants to look after (boring). So what's a restless, lonesome, post-abduction girl to do? She's going to bundle up in every layer imaginable and go for walks, so she can let the weather be a welcome distraction, until there are—temporarily—no aliens left in her brain, just thoughts about the cold, the wet, and possible frostbite. With enough cold, maybe I could go into a hibernation of sorts—emerge into the world sometime later, my whole self once more.

But for now, when I got home and stripped off all my winter things and defrosted, when it was just me and my thoughts again, no distractions—I missed him.

I missed him.

And Molly had been right, of course; the sting of Del's deception had faded. He should have told me straightaway that I was free to leave—but what was it he'd said?

I was afraid that you would leave. Afraid that you would not consider staying.

Any person with a heart could understand why he'd struggled to tell me.

So I went to work, and I came home, and I walked, and people kept looking at me concernedly. Sometimes, from the corner of my eye, I'd think I saw a flicker of swirling, familiar color slide across my darkened phone screen. There was never anything there, though, when I picked it up.

In the evenings, sometimes I'd close my bedroom door and bring out the sketchbook, tracing the graphite plants with a gentle finger. Remembering. And late at night, more and more

I lost my self-control and cried quietly into the darkness of my room.

There were no more unexpected house visits from Joe, and no texts, no calls—nothing. Molly did tell me she'd seen him again at Arlene's, looking morose over a beer; that Saturday she dragged me out there for burgers, and I half-expected to see him pouting in a booth, but he wasn't there.

Good—at least one of us might be feeling better.

Molly did most of the talking that evening—Kurt; her plans to redecorate her living room; speculation on whether Evan and Gabriella, now an item, were going to last. I really did try my best, smiling, responding when I was supposed to. I'd expected her to ask about Dale in Houston, but she didn't. No need for it; she could read me well enough.

That night when I got home, my dad was waiting up for me, watching an old Bobcats game in his recliner. Midge was snuggled next to him; she'd been his shadow ever since we'd come home. I couldn't blame her for being a bit sick of me.

I took a seat on the couch and watched the fourth quarter with him. It was a good game; we were up against the Griz, who we summarily demolished thirty-five to three. That's always nice to see.

Then the game was over, and an infomercial for cleaning supplies came on, and he turned down the volume, rather than be subjected to shouting about mops and dusters.

Neither one of us made to get up, though. I was just so *tired*. It was hard work, pretending that everything was fine all the time.

"You and the alien had some conversations, when you were there?"

I gave a little start. It wasn't anything I'd expected him to say. "Yes," I said, with some hesitation.

My dad took a breath, digesting that. He let the silence stretch out again. The mops and dusters were gone; now the guy was mute-yelling at us about cleaning solution. I watched as just one spritz eviscerated dirt, blood, mud. *Call now to claim this limited-time offer!*

Finally: "And he was a friendly sort of… person?"

I looked down at my lap. "Yes," I said again, softly. Then I stood up. "I'm going to bed. I—" Didn't actually have work tomorrow. And could tell I wouldn't fall asleep for hours still. "It's getting late."

He nodded at me. Smiled. "Right. Sleep well, hon."

"Thanks, Dad. You, too." We didn't say *I love you*s as often as some people, but that was what we meant.

He didn't move as I crossed the room, doing my damnedest not to look at him—just stayed in his recliner, watching the TV in that not-seeing kind of way. Some of the walls surrounding *that-thing-we-don't-talk-about* had been prodded at, poked aside.

But when one thing leaves, you can count on something new strutting around the bend to take its place. And this new thing was so strange, so terrifying, that it wasn't until very late indeed that I managed to fall asleep.

Chapter Seventeen

I JOLTED AWAKE INTO THE NEXT DAY, FLEEING A DREAM THAT had turned nightmarish. It had started off pleasant: wandering the ship, which in my dream state seemed more in its elegance and mystery to be a fairy castle. Rooms of secrets, rooms of wonder, with beautiful, shifting hallways running between them like veins.

Then coming to a plain room, very small, very square, with Del right in the middle. He stood with his head bowed, looking—not gaunt exactly, someone of his physique could never look gaunt, but… diminished. Desolate. And with the clarity dreams allow, it was clear that the space around him teemed with invisible monsters, crawling over the walls, slinking up from behind.

But that was all I knew. My dreams always leave me quickly.

Six a.m., my phone told me, after I'd taken a few deep breaths to shake off the uneasiness. Late to bed, early to rise— things were starting off well. It was Sunday, my free day.

Should have been a good feeling, but wasn't. There's less distraction in a day off.

I bit at my lip, considering whether I should text Ray and tell him I was coming in anyway. I'm sure he could find some task to throw at me that no one else in the shop wanted to do. Then again, working that many days in a row probably broke some labor laws. Plus coming in on my day off would seal the deal with everyone regarding the question of my sanity. Normal people didn't do that, and I was working on being normal.

So instead I pulled a paperback off the stack on my nightstand and tried to lose myself that way. An hour or so later, I heard my dad's usual breakfast-making clamor downstairs, so I left the paperback aside and went to take a shower.

When I came back in, wrapped in a towel, my phone's screen was a deep, grungy blue.

But no, it wasn't, I saw as I drew closer. The phone lay face up on my bedspread right where I'd left it charging, its screen perfectly dark and ordinary. Just to check if I had a notification, I flicked it on—nothing.

A strange reflection, some trick of the eye. I pulled on jeans and a T-shirt and went downstairs, toward the siren call of crackling bacon grease.

My dad and I kept our breakfast conversation light and careful—no mention of the topic we'd brushed against the night before, which was fine by me. The weather girl promised a balmy high of twenty-one and snow flurries. I'd read a bit more, I decided as I headed back upstairs, full on bacon and eggs. After that, I could tend to our houseplants, throw a load of laundry in the wash, then a walk…

All those plans fell away when I went back into my bedroom and saw my phone's screen awash with a sluggishly twisting dusty brown. It was the color of the underside of an old apricot, when it's gone soft and rotten.

Slowly, not taking my eyes off the phone, I shut the door behind me, waiting for the lock to click. Then I took a few steps forward, and a British woman's voice spoke to me through the phone's speakers.

"Corinne… My apologies for coming to you like this, out of the blue…"

Joanna sounded tired and tentative. And scared. A memory tugged at me, from when she'd woken me in the middle of the night. The night I'd discovered Del's old bedroom, devastated after the attack.

"You're here… how?" I asked. Which wasn't the smartest question I could have asked an entity that had digested the entire human Internet, but I was just so surprised.

"It's not difficult for me," she said. "My sincerest apologies once more. I know it must be a great shock to you…"

"No, no," I said, like you'd wave away a friend's concerns about imposing. Well, what else was I supposed to say? *Please go away?* Not that I felt like that. Underneath my surprise, really I was glad to see her.

"You've been well?" she asked.

I hesitated. "Well enough. What's happened?" Because something must have happened, for her to come to me this way.

Her coils throbbed. "The master is unwell."

"Sick?" I asked with a pulse of alarm.

"He is… not himself. He's only keeping me on in my most rudimentary capacities, to maintain basic ship functions. He's locked me out."

"Locked you out of the whole ship?" I asked, disbelieving.

Her brown went dark and muddy. "Yes," she replied, her voice small. "All the parts that count."

"What about Jexrah? Meervit?"

She quivered. "Gone. He sent them away."

"But…" I frowned. "So he's just there, by himself? What's he doing?"

"He—" Tiny white dots bloomed on the screen, and her coils jerked and shuddered beneath them. "I'm not free to answer that. Maybe—" Another sprinkling of white dots, fine as flour, as her loyalty fought against her. "No. Not possible."

"Don't push yourself," I said hastily. "But can you tell me *why* he's acting this way?"

Her silence was answer enough.

"Okay," I said, taking a deep breath. "Okay. Then what do I need to do?"

She shriveled, grew even darker. "Would you come back to us, Corinne, to help him? Please. I… I am begging you."

I went still, both body and brain. Back to the *Huivnarrut*, leaving everything behind again?

"My dad. My friends… my job…" But even as the words left my lips, conviction had already come over me, tight as a clenched fist. The answer to Joanna's question was obvious.

Of course I would go back for him.

"You are Ambassador status now," she said. "It allows you to come and go from the ship as you please. From Tenctah as well."

"Good," I said absentmindedly, as I went to my dresser and pulled out a thick wool sweater. I'd need to bundle up for my walk in the woods. "Is the ship still in the same spot?"

"You mean you'll come back?" A trace of orange bled into her coloring.

"Yes. But what about the ship?"

"It's still there. I can guide you."

I rooted through my sock drawer, pulling out my fuzziest pair. It seemed to me that my reality ten minutes ago—breakfast, the weather girl, our kitchen—was a different universe, adjacent to the one I was in now. That girl from before was a husk, filled with nothing but yearning silence. Now excitement stirred in my chest, mixed with an alarm for Del that made my whole body ache. I was full to the brim, and it was time to go.

All my warm stuff donned, I ripped a page from my sketchbook and grabbed a pencil. I dashed off a note to my dad just in case, then stuck it in the front of the sketchbook and laid that right in the middle of my bed. It wasn't anything that would arouse suspicion on first glance, but if I took a while to come back and my dad grew worried, no doubt he'd find the note.

Then I picked Joanna up and headed downstairs. I could hear my dad watching TV in the other room. "Going for a walk!" I called, and he made a sound that said he'd heard me.

By now he was used to me and my private bubble of subdued sadness; my long walks were standard operating procedure.

After this, I'd be lucky if he ever let me out of the house again. But I'd cross that bridge when I came to it.

Then I left out our back door, sans Midge this time but with Joanna tucked in my chest coat pocket.

The promised snowflakes had already started their downward drift, and the air held that singular winter hush. Joanna was mercifully silent. From the driveway on the other side of the house came the crunch of tires on gravel. A car door slammed. *Dad must be heading to the store*, I thought.

I was in such a state it never occurred to me that those last two sounds should have been reversed—that they were not the sounds of my dad leaving, but rather of someone driving up to our house.

Within a minute I made it across the meadow and plunged into the woods. I didn't run, but I was sure hustling, which is hard enough to do in the snow.

In my mind, I was returning to that night Joanna had woken me up "to check on him," as she'd put it, her anxiety obvious. I'd found Del soundly slumbering on the sim-room floor, under the soporific influence of the gas, and what had I made of the situation? Laughed it off as him having a bit too much of his own private fun. Who wouldn't do the same, with a magical toy like a sim room?

Afterwards I'd found his bedroom and thrown a hunk of

rubble at Joanna when she'd refused to divulge a single secret and then I'd just been so mad at her that the first part of that strange night hadn't seemed so important.

But maybe I should have given more thought as to *why* Joanna had been so panicked.

I pulled her out of my coat pocket as I kept up my brisk pace. She was back to that sad, dusty brown color. "Listen," I said, "I don't know if you can tell me this—well, I know you won't be able to tell me anything for certain, since Del's revoked your ship access—but do you think he's in the sim room? Is that what you're really worried about?"

"I…" She brightened a hair. "Actually, I *can* answer that question. I'm forbidden to give you anything definite, but speculation should be fine. And yes, that is my fear. You'd best head a little more to the left."

I adjusted my course. "All right. Now that night you woke me up to check on Del, there was a smell—that gas that gets pumped into the air during simulations. Whatever dispenses the gas had broken, so…" I trailed off as an obvious thought occurred. "Hang on—had *he* turned the gas up high?"

"I'm not at liberty to answer that."

Seemed to me that she *would* have the liberty if the answer were no. Which meant that yes, it probably had been Del himself who'd turned the gas up beyond its standard levels. "Give me an overview on the gas," I said, putting her back in my pocket.

"It's called"—here she rattled off some long chemical name,

which I promptly forgot—"and in low doses it's quite harm-less. Its primary use is as an immersive aid."

"What about in higher doses?"

She stilled. "In higher doses it gives the same effect to those who breathe it, but in a more intense way. One could become so locked in the moment that there are effects on one's memory—a forgetting of anything that has no bearing on the here and now. People frequently mention a loss of their sense of time; so much immersion means one won't be able to keep a schedule in mind. But fortunately these effects have been demonstrated to be temporary. After the gas dissipates, there are no long-lasting effects on the brain."

I nodded, turning her words over as I tramped around a thicket. That night, Del and I had spent some length of time spooning on the floor—nine minutes or so, if I remembered Joanna's words correctly, and I'd been shocked to hear it. There was no doubt in my mind now that the gas had played some part in my confusion.

Still, these were temporary effects; Joanna had said so her-self. *Well, that doesn't sound so bad*, I was about to say, but then she continued on, her voice grave.

"You should know, though, that in yet higher doses the gas can become hazardous. One's focus might become mis-placed—concentrating on housework while the house burns down around you, for example. Crucially, those under the in-fluence might fall unconscious, rendering them unable to move to a safer area. Should the parts per million stay at a high level, in this sleep state one might achieve such focus that the body can be tricked into thinking that essential physical functions are still occurring." She paused. "One might forget to keep breathing."

One might… Del might. I hastened my steps. "Let me talk this through," I said to her, "and you don't have to say a thing. Here's what it sounds like to me… Del's been spending a lot of time in the sim room, and he's been cranking up the gas. And the reason for this is because he wants to be fully immersed in something that he's doing in the sim room. And that something is… er… well, it can't be good." Something shameful? My mind flicked to the obvious answer of sexual fantasies—oh *God*, was he simulating me?—but that simply didn't mesh with who I believed Del to be.

I picked my way down a little hill, thinking hard. What unsavory things might you use a sim room for? The possibilities were unnervingly endless. Vengeance, violence, sexual deviance… but again, not one of those made sense to me. Del wasn't like that. A nebulous answer danced just beyond the outskirts of my mind, taunting me.

"He wants to be immersed," I whispered to myself, "and to forget. Forget what? Oh, Del…" All I could think about was his breath leaving him as he lay in that horrid lower level, with its shadows, and his sad, plain bedroom, and his original, ruined bedroom, and whatever demons he had summoned to keep him company.

The original bedroom… destroyed by what's-his-name, the competing heir…

"Oh no," I breathed.

Because hadn't I had a similar thought, that first time Del had shown me the sim room? *Oh, I could be Elizabeth Bennet, or fly over the Grand Canyon, or go to space… or see my mother again.*

"It's something to do with the death of his bodyguard, isn't it?" I said. All around us was the crystalline rustle of snowflakes settling.

Joanna said nothing.

"Some sort of revenge on—on Ahmpo," I said, finally remembering the other heir's name, "or maybe Del's going back to times before his guard died. Happier times." Would he really torment himself that way? A sick feeling swirled within me at the thought.

"Khindrae Meervit related to you what happened," Joanna asked, "before we came to Earth?"

"Yes, yes. Aren't we nearly there?"

"Just a ways up—" *Ahead,* I knew she wanted to finish, but I'd twisted around with a gasp at an unexpected noise from behind me. A human noise, not that far away. Someone had sneezed?

No one there that I could see. But there were fir trees all around, and snow clouded the air; it wasn't like I could see far in any direction.

"There's a cell-phone signal back the way we came," Joanna murmured. "Maybe fifty feet behind us. The number is registered to a Joe Gagnon, twenty-seven years old. You know him, I believe."

Of all the times for Joe to snap, it had had to happen now. Cold fear brushed against me. Lord knew what he planned to do, following me out into the woods like this.

"Turn around and keep walking," she said firmly, and I did. "You don't have a weapon on you or anything, do you?"

"No," I said softly, and took stock of what I did have on me that could be of use. Precisely nothing was the answer. "I—I think I'll just keep moving, act like I don't know he's there."

"A good plan, I'd say. The ship isn't far off. A minute or two more and we'll be there."

A thought stole my breath away. "Can you check on my dad with his phone? Is he—?"

"Seems to be all right. I think his phone's in his back pocket; he's moving around. I don't hear anything out of the ordinary."

So Joe hadn't hurt him, or at least not badly. A possibility occurred to me. "You can't, like, zap Joe through his phone, can you? Or something?"

"Not in this temperature. Well, not in a reasonable amount of time."

It had been worth a shot. "Joanna, I have to get to Del. There's no time to give Joe the runaround." But that meant Joe was about to witness me get vacuumed up by an alien space-ship. Not ideal.

"I suppose it can't be helped," she said unhappily. She was just as anxious as I was for me to get back on the ship. "You're almost there. You'll cross the pulse screen in about twenty feet."

"Pulse screen?"

She sighed. "You probably hit it your first time coming aboard? It's an animal deterrent, causes momentary blindness. You'll feel some tingling for a second. I'd turn it off for you, if my restrictions allowed."

I'd nearly forgotten that part of the abduction. "Great. Oh, Joanna, I didn't even think—what if he follows me up—?"

But I didn't hear her answer, because I'd hit the pulse screen, my world had gone white-violet, my skin had lit up with tingles, and Joe had called out to me.

The one plus was that I'd been braced as much as I could for the pulse screen, so this time I didn't fall forward into the snow from shock. I wrenched around toward the sound of Joe's voice. I was about to give him the show of a lifetime.

"Corinne!" he called again, his voice a rasp.

"Why are you following me?"

He didn't deign to reply, of course. Joe was the one with all the answers, and who was *I* to question him? The girl wants to break up? Pretend it's not happening. Everyone says she's experiencing real mental distress from the breakup? Convince yourself it's just a temporary split. Her father says not to come around anymore? Stop by unannounced and follow her into the woods.

"What are you doing out here?" he asked. I could hear the tramp of his boots in the snow as he moved closer. "I heard you talking to yourself, talking a lot…"

My surroundings were a wash of white. The air was thickening, but gravity still held me firmly to the earth.

I took another step backward. "Just taking a walk. Thinking out loud."

"You know what they say about people who talk a lot to themselves." He made a strained noise, almost a laugh. It wasn't any sort of noise you'd make if you had your head on right. "You think too much, Corinne. Trip yourself up that way. Lose sight of a good thing. If you just *loosened up*—"

"Joe…"

More crunching in snow. He must be just at the edge of the pulse screen, about to cross through. "He's close," said Joanna in a minute voice, and I fell back another step.

She didn't escape Joe's attention, though. "What was that?" he asked roughly, and I thought of glass cracking in a man's fist, splinters burrowing into skin. "What is this place? This snow…"

"Don't come any closer!"

"Can't you even fucking look at me when I'm talking to you? Why aren't you looking at me? I'm out here for you, you fucking cunt. Look at me. *Look at me!*"

But I couldn't see him yet; my surroundings held the blurred mistiness of a Bob Ross painting, before he's added in all the happy little trees. I heard the mad, forward dash of boots through snow, then Joe's cry of surprise when he hit the pulse screen. But before he'd crossed he had launched himself towards me, and he hit me like a linebacker, pushing me down into the snow, pushing me deep—*how long had it been since I'd made a snow angel?*—this large, furious, crazed man pinning me down…

Until he wasn't. Gravity fell away, and he peeled away from me. I could see him now, a little, wriggling in the air above me as if he were a marionette on strings, controlled by a puppeteer on high.

The cloaked underbelly of the ship was sucking me upward, too. Snow, mashed into my hair, was falling out in clumps to hit the ground several yards below. My whole back side was freezing and sodden.

Joe was maybe eight feet higher than me; he would make it onto the ship first. He writhed in midair, shouting, cursing—more a thing wild than a man. The *Huivnarrut* was fully functioning this time around, so the approaching, glittering vortex of the ship's underbelly was invisible. From Joe's perspective, it must seem like God Himself had crooked a finger to usher the both of us up into the heavens.

And wouldn't it be nice if God could just take over from here? I sagged, not fighting the unfaltering force that drew me ever upwards. But this reprieve was temporary; Joe would make it onto the ship first, I thought again. He would drop onto the ship, and then I would join him seconds later. Me and this hulking madman, together in the snug portal room. I had the advantage of knowing what was about to happen. Physically, though, Joe had all the advantage over me.

Except that I would be the second person to enter the room.

Any plan, however malformed, was better than no plan at all. I gathered my knees into my chest, interlocking my fingers tightly around them (this was good, because it stopped them shaking), then glanced up toward Joe. Joanna was saying something to me, but I couldn't hear her over his bellowing.

This part of the process I had never seen before, and I watched on in dazed fascination. Joe was there one second, and then he'd popped out of existence, like a stage magician had magicked him away. Just a few seconds more and then I would be the one doing the disappearing act.

I whispered a shaky little prayer into the open air. The sky above me blurred, stretched, the ship's illusion breaking. Darkness filtered in, and now that swirling, windy pressure... I cinched my fingers harder around my legs, tucking in my chin, tight as a roly-poly. Up was up no longer, the world a shadowed, confused limbo...

Del, I'm coming. Hold on for me.

Then I was plunging down to the portal-room floor, cannonballing onto Joe like this were some happier, carefree time, us at a pool party, not him a man obsessed and me a woman desperate.

I collided with his shoulder, garnering a roar of male outrage, but no time to look; my arm was already outstretched for the silver door button.

The door whooshed open. "Corinne," he called, already behind me as I staggered out of the portal room.

And swayed on my feet for a moment, gaping. The hallway before me was an unrelenting, grimy red all the way up and down, the inner walls of a dying artery.

I'm coming! Hold on—

But sudden pressure at my ankle, the feel of fingers clawing at me... and the wet soles of my snow boots were slick on the polished floor, which came up fast to meet me, smacking my knees, arms, right cheek. I croaked a gasp, no air left in my lungs.

Joe's grip on my boot tightened, and I could hear him moving behind me.

"So," he said. "This is your Houston?"

Chapter Eighteen

I KICKED BACKWARD WITH EVERYTHING I HAD, AND I COULD have cried with happiness when I felt my boot connect. The kick wasn't hard enough to do any real damage, but it certainly caught him off guard. Joe's hand fell away, and I scrabbled at the ground, fingers sliding over cold, smooth floor.

Found a purchase. Lurched to my feet, then stumbled onward, as fast as I could manage.

Joe was close, though; I could hear his lumbering footsteps behind me. I knew the ship well, had walked its halls in my dreams, but with this silty, nightmarish red all around, the doors to either side were strange to me.

Except, as I rounded a corner, for one door, with its familiar map of the ship emblazoned beside it on the wall. That map shone through the red like a lighthouse through a storm.

The elevator.

Miracle of miracles, the door swished open obligingly when I hammered the bottom floor of the diagram. I sped inside, praying I'd run fast enough that Joe hadn't seen me come in here, knowing that he probably had. He'd find me soon enough.

But if I could just turn off the gas in the meantime…

"Cover your mouth and nose," Joanna said in clipped tones from my pocket, and I pulled the neck of my coat up, with my eyes peeking out over top. It was a good thing she'd said something; the cloying musk of the gas nearly bowled me over when the door opened again a second later, never mind my makeshift mask.

The walls of Del's quarters were lit with the same muddy sanguine color as upstairs. Shadows clung thickly to the corners, the dark orb light overhead paying no attention to my entrance.

Anxiety wrapped around me like a vice as I hastened over to the sim-room door. I watched my hand float out and hit the little silver button.

The brightness of the room within was in stark contrast to the rest of Del's quarters. The scene inside was just the same as that other night: the gold-smeared floor rippling sickly, the noxious gas permeating every inch of air, and Del, goggled and comatose, in the middle of it all.

He was very still.

Then a male voice said something gruffly in Ziryahshun— no one there, just the simulation talking—and Del's lips twitched a little in response.

I flew over to him, ripping the goggles from his eyes. "How do I—?" And Joanna, anticipating me, was already shouting the words at me from my pocket, which I parroted to the room. Something in the walls clicked. The simulated person said no more. The roiling floor calmed. Vaguely, I thought of invisible demons circling us, hissing, spitting, sneering, only to melt away into the ether.

"That's done it," Joanna said as I clung to Del, watching the too slow rise and fall of his chest. A strange, not unpleasant pressure was building in my head. My fingertips were tingling.

But what did any of that matter? Del was all right. He was going to be okay. His face looked drawn along the edges, pulled tight, and I traced his thin lips with my finger, then lowered my head to lay it against his, felt the russet velvet of his cheek on my own, tangled my hand in the heavy scraggle of his hair.

Was I forgetting something? Couldn't be—I'd done what I'd come for.

"Corinne?" called a familiar voice from somewhere not too far away.

"Corinne," hissed another familiar voice, this one female, from my pocket. She sounded scared. Why was my coat up over my nose?

"I know you're here somewhere," said the other voice. Male.

"You can't let Joe find you in here," said the woman.

I pondered that strange sentence. It sounded like something that made sense.

"Come out," called the man.

"I want you to run," said the woman. "You're going to run out this door, and the elevator's right there. You hear me? That's what you have to do to save Del, because if you don't, Joe's going to find the both of you in here, and then who knows what he'll do."

"The elevator."

"Yes. Now."

So I rose begrudgingly to my feet, away from the still-slumbering Del, when all I wanted was to watch for his next breath, to remind myself of the essence of him, all those details that had run away from me in my time away…

"Hurry!" said the woman—Joanna was her name. *"The elevator!"*

"Fine, fine," I grumbled. Then I gathered whatever spare concentration I could muster—very little—and burst from the room. I'd like to think I did Joanna proud; I did reach the elevator in time, even remembered to punch the button for the next floor up. A dark-haired man I knew—Joe—was in Del's bedroom across the way, and he poked his head out as the elevator door closed. I almost stuck my tongue out at him, then remembered that Joanna had said something about him being dangerous.

I nearly started crying when the elevator deposited me a second later back into the diseased red corridor. This wasn't right, none of it was right, and God, how I missed Del. What if Joe didn't follow me up straightaway and found him downstairs?

"What if Joe finds Del downstairs?"

"He cares about you, not him. Now you run, Corinne—*run!*" For the elevator door had swept closed behind me again. With the fresher air, more sense rushed back to me, and with it came a sensible terror that I wouldn't be alone for much longer; the elevator was too damn fast, just another magical gadget in this floating castle of wonders. Give it a few seconds, and Joe would be here.

I ran.

And footsteps joined mine a moment later—the pounding, heavy footfalls of a very angry man. There was no time to form a plan, no time for anything but running away—and he would catch me soon enough.

But a door up ahead called to me like an old friend.

Into the hothouse I plunged.

I had left one nightmare, only to enter a new one. The hothouse was dimmer than I'd ever seen, the white stone path a dingy strip barely visible for the dark, uneven splotches littering it. And the smell… I lifted my eyes and saw that the lights in the ceiling were choked with fleshy, bilious yellow flowers and vines upon vines, some thick as my wrist, others a mess of fine tendrils, spidering in every direction.

The thicker vines bowed with dark, bulging shapes. Something plummeted to the ground just before me, smashing, water balloon-like, with a wet, meaty smack.

My humble little tomato plants, now thick as kudzu, had overrun the whole room.

A hiss of air from behind me: the door. The sound was just enough warning for me to dive off the path into the overgrowth.

It embraced me. Vines furry with white hairs caught at my hair and my clothes. Glossy tomato skin, riddled with stretch marks from malignant growth, brushed against my cheek. Wetness overhead dripped on my head in pregnant, seed-filled globs. Thick rivulets of the stuff slid through my hair and pooled around my ear, before continuing a slow descent down my neck.

But my quick action had sufficed. Backlit in red, Joe dashed through the door and came to a stunned halt just a few steps from me. I watched, not daring to breathe, as he clapped a hand to his mouth and swallowed back a retch. He had always picked the tomatoes off his burgers, I seemed to remember.

The door whisked shut, the red gash of light from the hallway beyond thinning to a crimson needle—then gone completely. Warm, dripping darkness closed around us, tight as a fist, the overhead lights providing just the barest amount of light to see. I swore I could hear the inching creak of things growing.

"Corinne!" Joe called, taking a few wobbly steps down the path. Fear tinged the anger in his voice. What must he think of the *Huivnarrut*? "I know you're in here."

I watched on as he moved further down the path and eventually slipped around the bend. Then I reached into my coat's chest pocket, snarling silently when a tangle of vines caught at my sleeve.

"Joanna," I breathed, bringing the phone to my mouth. "Stay quiet. Don't light up. But you're still there, right?"

"I'm here," came her tiny reply.

"Good. I'm in the hothouse. It's a real sight in here." I loosed a breath, quietly. Steeled myself for what seemed to inevitably come next. "You still can't control the ship, right?"

"Corinne!" Joe called again from somewhere off to the left.

"Right," said Joanna.

No holding cells, then, that I could have her operate and somehow lock him up. It was a large enough ship that I might be able to sneak out of here, continue our game of hide-and-seek.

But he was liable to hurt me if he found me, I knew.

I closed my eyes. "Do you remember when I asked you if you could zap Joe? And you said no, not given the temperature. But it's warm in here, so could you—?"

"His phone isn't on board," she said, and I felt like strangling someone. "It's down on the ground. He must have lost it during the ascent."

All right. Think. "Are there weapons on board?"

"Locked up."

"Okay," I said, even though all of this was distinctly not okay. "Then… what about this phone? My phone?"

"I… could. But it's not going to be anything that will really incapacitate. It won't be some sort of huge explosion."

And with that last word, one thought kick-started the next, and I gripped the phone hard. "You could make a spark, though? A flame?"

"Yes…? Oh, Corinne. What *else* do you have in this room?"

"Never mind about that. Could you do it on command?"

"It will take me a few minutes," she said, sounding supremely unhappy. "It's going to destroy the phone; I won't have a way to talk to you afterwards. Are you sure?"

"Yes," I said, sticking her back in my pocket, then snuck a step to my left. A cluster of overripe tomatoes burst and squished against my side like bubble wrap. I bit my lip hard and maintained a forward creep.

My chest pocket was starting to feel nice and toasty. Movement between two vine-festooned trees caught my eye through the gloom: Joe's head on a swivel, devilish in the dark. He was searching for me, knew I was still here. My eyes traveled down to his hand; he was holding something. A familiar shape, an item from distant, happier times—my metal gardening trowel, with its sharp, pointed tip. He was gripping it like you would a knife.

And then Joe began talking to me, as he kept prowling. "Corinne"—he stepped out of sight again—"won't you come out and tell me all about it? This place. This is where you actually went, isn't it?"

I bit back a yell as my right foot came down on a tomato big as a pumpkin and pierced through the skin, straight into rotting, watery guts. If I got out of this alive, I would never eat another tomato as long as I lived.

"I understand it now," he continued. "I didn't before, but I do now. You were abducted. Aliens. God, who'd ever believe it? But babe, *I understand*. I've seen it now. You just have to trust me; I'll take you out of this place. Help you heal."

Before me, just visible in the dim light, was the dried-out husk of the gohrrow plant. Interwoven vines draped over one side of it like a curtain, the fuzz of their hair matted together, but I'd still recognize the gohrrow's rotund pitcher belly anywhere.

I dropped to my knees and rooted through the dirt just beside the gohrrow plant, feeling for—there!—cool metal. Shivering despite the heat, I lifted the precious, fabricated metal tumbler out of the dirt. I brushed its screw-top clean and loosed a relieved sigh when I peeked inside; the interior was empty and bone-dry.

Standing back up, I heard movement somewhere to the left. Joe was closer than I'd thought. It was hard to keep track of where he was, with the low light and the vegetable monstrosity all around.

"What'd they do to you?" he said. "Did they"—he made a noise almost like a laugh, then turned it into a cough—"probe you?"

The vines were obstructing the opening of the gohrrow plant's hollow pitcher trap. Shuddering, I began picking them off. The vine hairs left a foul slick of oil on my fingers. My pocket was starting to feel uncomfortably hot.

"I'm sure they did something to you," Joe was saying, "the way you've been looking since you got back. Like your fucking dog died. They must've done something, huh?"

The last vine cleared, I thrust my arm all the way down into the pitcher trap and rooted around. For one terrible second my fingers brushed only empty air. Then my hand knocked into something dry and lumpy, and with trembling fingers I lifted out the clump of dried gunpowder I'd stashed there in my moment of clairvoyance. Jexrah had destroyed the materials in the gazebo, but she hadn't found the gunpowder itself.

Little pieces of the dark ball were flaking off in my palm. I started mashing the ball between my hands into a floury powder, before dumping it all into the tumbler. Then I wiped my hands on my jeans and fished my phone from my pocket. It was nearly too hot to touch, the back of the phone bulging disturbingly.

And a single spark from static electricity can set things off! I remembered my professor saying. I gritted my teeth, gingerly placed the phone in the tumbler alongside the gunpowder, sealed the lid tight, then turned in the direction of the stone path.

"Stuff like that'll make a girl get all fucked in the head," Joe said. He was out of sight—somewhere near the gazebo, from the sound of it. "I'll get us out of here. I'll help you forget all about it. Just come out, babe, so we can talk."

And I took a shaking, quiet step onto the path. Heart hammering, I laid the tumbler—the bomb—at my feet. Then I made to head back into the safety of the overgrowth, when Joe's voice stopped me in my tracks.

"There you are!" he said from behind me, all jovial, like the two of us were in on some hilarious inside joke.

I turned back around. He had emerged from around the bend, looking calm as could be. His hands were empty, but no doubt he had the trowel on him somewhere.

I'm sure I looked just gorgeous, all covered in tomato gunk. "Here I am," I said, rearranging my lips into some approximation of a smile, trying to project an aura of someone gentle and trusting. Lord, what I wouldn't give to have the luxury of being someone gentle and trusting right now.

He started toward me at a slow stroll, and I couldn't help taking a step backward. He stopped, throwing up his hands like he was calming a skittish horse. He was still too far away from the tumbler. "No need to run," he said. "I'm going to get you out of here."

Be loving and gentle and kind. "I'd like that."

He came forward another step, too much white around his eyes. "Will you tell me how it happened?"

"A walk in the woods." *Trusting and doe-eyed and placid.* "It was awful."

"I'm sure it was," he said, unblinking. He moved another step forward. "But you came back here. Why would you do that?"

Oh God. "I…" Shaking my head. Just a silly, silly girl, doing silly, silly things. "I just thought…"

"It wouldn't have anything to do with that monster downstairs, would it?"

I froze, and of course he could see the truth in my eyes.

"That *is* it," he said softly.

"Did you hurt him?" All pretense falling away.

"Maybe I'll let you find out, after I knock some sense into you." And he lunged for me as I jerked away, screaming Joanna's name.

There was a horrible, loud pop, followed by a burst of white-orange flame, which briefly illuminated the mutant surroundings. A blurred shard of something rocketed past my temple. Shrieks from behind me, which dampened to bleating whimpers—then a shape in the darkness hurtled towards me, past me… towards Joe.

A roar, a final scream, and I knew he was dead. There was a terrible odor in the air—the smell of things charred and blackened to a crisp, mixed with a seared tomato tang.

The world swayed around me. No, I was swaying. Falling.

But Del was there to catch me before I hit the ground.

Chapter Nineteen

THERE HAD BEEN QUITE A FEW TIMES RECENTLY WHEN I'D COME to in a bed, fuzzy on how I'd ended up there. As I swam back towards consciousness this time around, I resolved to make an effort to live more carefully. Fewer panic attacks, less maht-drinking, less black powder.

Being carried back to my bed in a pleasure-induced stupor by my lover, though—that was all right. That I wouldn't mind repeating.

Del was the first thing I saw when I opened my eyes, brooding in the bedside armchair. The wall behind him was a washed-out, uneasy mauve—but at least there was no more of that awful red.

"Hey there," I murmured, and Del was out of the armchair in an instant. He stood beside the bed, positively coursing with energy, ready to Do Something Useful—but the last time I'd seen him (our day of revelations) I had been so angry and hurt that of course he didn't know where we stood with each other.

"Sit here," I said, nodding at the space beside me on the bed, and he settled beside me, moving oh-so-gently. I snuggled into him and realized I was naked. He was not, unfortunately.

"My clothes…?"

He motioned to a pile on the floor. I could see at a glance that they were ruined. The tomato muck liberally coating them would have come out in the wash, but it had bubbled and blackened from the heat of the bomb.

"I had to check you over for injuries," he explained. "But there were no punctures, no serious burns. Some slight scalding on your left calf and thigh, it seems, but that's all. You were very lucky. The man—Joe—was not."

My stomach twisted. "Was it very bad?"

"Yes," he said plainly. He gave me a look that was… watchful. "Would you like to know?"

"I…" I looked down at my hands—these hands that had pounded the ingredients into powder, measured out the magic ratio, mixed them together, cradled the dusty concoction in my palm like treasure, then poured my treasure into the tumbler. If I had done all that, the least I could do was have enough guts to hear the aftermath. "Tell me."

He took a long moment to speak. Finally, "One shard through his right eye." He spoke as calmly as you'd relate today's weather's highs and lows. "Another glanced the side of his neck, and one more through his left hand. The neck wound was the fatal wound of the three. He would not have lasted long. All I did was spare him more suffering."

"Oh," I said in a small voice, as my eye, my hand, and my

neck lit up with phantom tingles. I huddled in closer to him. "Oh, I see."

"Corinne, you are not bad for having defended yourself." He shifted to look at me, his red eyes grave. "You could easily have been killed, though. A weapon like that is too rudimentary, too unpredictable. Will you promise me—?"

"No more bombs," I said, hugging his arm, and I was crying now, a steady, sorry flow of tears. Because despite Joe's attempted assault—and, probably, murder—I had also known a different part of him, a part I'd believed essentially good, and it was shocking to know that that part of him was gone, too— and by my hands, at that.

So I cried, then cried some more, until I felt like a wet rag that's had every last drop of water wrung out of it.

Then I looked back up at Del, who had borne all these tears in comforting silence, a steady tree trunk at my side. "But you're okay."

"That I am. Because you came back."

"To save you." I looked him square on, felt my whole body do a sigh of relief. "I think it was a close thing. You looked very… dead-ish." I wasn't over today's events, not by a long shot, but I could feel the festering hurt that had plagued me these past weeks scabbing up, beginning to shrivel away into nothingness.

Probably there would be a trace of a scar left. But just a pale, little, white one. A scar to remind me of things I'd left behind.

His hold around me tightened. I thought of wood nymphs melting into their oak trees as human men prowled through the forest. "Saving the heir is a serious thing," my tree rumbled.

"Is it?"

"It is. I owe you an act."

"Very medieval, isn't it? Surely there's no need."

"No," he said, in a tone that allowed no argument. "I owe you an act, whether now or in the future."

"What sort of act?"

"That decision lies with you."

All righty then. Probably it was best to just accept that a powerful alien prince was vowing to do me a big favor. That might not be such a bad thing.

"I could always put in a word with my mother for a royal commendation," he said. "Saving the vra-khinahar would certainly seem to merit it." I looked over at him and was relieved to see he was joking.

"Hush, you," I said and gave him a kiss. Then we kissed some more. Then he held me as I closed my eyes and told myself to fall asleep, all while visions of the hothouse spun through my mind—fire, flames, a body ruined by flying scraps of metal.

It's a wonder I ever fell asleep, but I did.

When I woke up next, Del was dead asleep and spooning me. He had one arm draped around me, tugging me in close; the other arm was snaked under me, his hand at my breast. Men of any species have their basic similarities, I guess.

It was tempting to just stay put, but… Really there were too many *buts* to list. The back of my tongue tasted like explosion.

My hair was giving off whiffs of roasted tomatoes. Probably I had seeds in my ear.

More seriously, I had work tomorrow, my dad was no doubt out of his mind with worry, and a deceased man's truck was parked in our driveway. This time around, I refused to simply vanish into the ether that was "Houston."

"Time?" I asked in a whisper. My voice was hoarse. I suppose I really had screamed for Joanna quite loudly.

"Still Sunday, about one in the afternoon," she said softly, so as not to disturb The Master.

Good—that left me enough time for whatever came next. I slithered out of Del's hold on me and tiptoed to the bathroom.

"You're all… restored?" I asked her as I ran the bath. How much soap do you need to cleanse away the memory of monster tomatoes dripping their overripe innards all over you? I turned my three favorite knobs up to the max.

Joanna wiggled peachily. "I am. It's good to be back."

"It didn't hurt to explode the phone, did it?"

"Oh no, not at all. You're just sort of there, then not there."

"Well, that's good." I sank into the bath with a weary sigh. The floral-scented bubbles were doing a decent job masking the tomato scent, but I had a sneaking suspicion it would only be a temporary fix. Would people be able to smell the tomatoes on me tomorrow? I could tell them I'd been sprayed by a skunk and had to take a tomato bath. A skunk in January. Yeah, right.

After I'd scrubbed myself down three or four times, Joanna spoke up again. "I have something to tell you."

Uh-oh, I thought, then saw she was all twists of lavender and gold. "What's that?"

"The master has asked me to implement some changes. The first being that my responsibility to you is increased. Starting today, I will provide you the same level of service I do for him; I'm speaking of security, analysis, et cetera. In terms of informational confidence, anything shared with the master in my presence should be considered as something you may also know—and I will be sure to keep you up-to-date on what you *should* know. I am now an open book to you, so to speak. You may also dismiss me whenever you please. As for the *Huivnarrut*, there are no longer any parts that are off-limits to you. The ship's movements are under the master's command only, but should he be killed or incapacitated, command shifts immediately to yourself."

"Well!" I said, light-headed.

But Joanna wasn't finished yet. "The master has also instructed me to deposit a sum of money into your bank account, which I have done. No one will ever come knocking, so to speak, about this money. Should you ever require more, all you need to do is ask. When you're ready, you and I can come up with a story that explains your good fortune, and I will lay whatever record-keeping groundwork is necessary to support that story, should anyone you know find out about your windfall."

Windfall? "How much money?"

"Three million dollars, give or take. As I said, we can easily supply you more. But I thought that a decent amount to start."

It was a lucky thing I didn't faint and drown in the bath. "Is that... say that again?"

"Approximately three million dollars has been deposited into your—Corinne?" For I'd rocketed to my feet, splashing the bath water everywhere. I grabbed a towel and stomped back into the bedroom.

Del was out of bed and over by the fabricator, which was chugging away making something. "What's all this three-million-dollars business?" I snapped at him, and he swung around, looking alarmed. Well, he ought to be alarmed! I would have had my hands on my hips, but, alas, I needed them to keep my towel up. I was mad, but I didn't know why.

"And—and I'm captain of the ship if you *die*?" I continued. "Second-in-command? It's just, I didn't ask you to—not to say I'm not flattered—great for my resume—but... here's the thing." Did I know the thing? No, not really, but if I kept talking maybe I'd work it out. "Joanna says she's an open book to me now—that's fantastic, huge improvement—but... but... why's *she* telling me this?" There it was; I'd finally figured it out. "Del, I can't stand all these secrets. I hate being left in the dark. So to do all that, with the money and the ship, and not to tell me—to have her tell me instead..." The fabricator dinged. "What's that?"

"It's not important," he said quickly, making to walk over to me. "Let's discuss this first."

"No, stop that. You see, you're doing it right there. Just tell me what's in the fabricator."

He paused, in an unhappy sort of way. "It's a weapon for you," he said. "Something small and reliable for you to keep on your person."

I brought my hands to my face, rubbed my eyes with the heels of my palms, then felt the towel slipping down. I hiked it back up again. This was really no way to have such a critical conversation. "See, that *is* important, though." I could feel myself starting to come down from the anger high. But I was still very, very frustrated. "What I mean is that this—you and me—is a big enough challenge as it is. I want to make it work. I think I'm prepared for that—well, as prepared as I can be. But I have to know what's going on; it's just not going to work otherwise. Your sisters can run political circles around me, and I assume everyone else you know can too, so you have to let me in on things. Not Joanna. *You.*"

He'd crossed the room to stand before me. It was shocking how much better I felt when he was close to me, mad or not. "That all makes sense," he said.

"It—it does?"

"Yes. Next time I'll come to you first, not her."

I opened my mouth again on an impulse. "Del, are you expecting to die soon?"

He frowned down at me. "This question because you would assume command of the ship, if that were to happen?"

"Well, yes."

"Death is something one in my position thinks of often. It's part of the role, unfortunately." His frown deepened. "I'm afraid that I might be a difficult person to… date? Is that the correct term?"

I had to smile. "Yes. And also yes. It may come as a surprise, but it hasn't exactly escaped me that dating you will pose some unique challenges."

"And you're sure?" he said, eyeing me closely. "About… dating?"

"I am," I said, surprising myself with how firm my voice was. I walked over and sat on the edge of the bed. He took a seat beside me.

"But you have concerns."

"That, yes, and questions." A whole heap of them, tall enough to climb to the moon.

"Ask me."

You couldn't tell he was used to commanding people, could you? "Well, there's my family and my friends and my job," I said, ticking these off on my fingers. "I can't just jet off to Tenctah and never come home again."

"Snap travel should allow for fairly quick travel between Earth and Tenctah. Joanna's found a route she estimates will take an average of three hours."

"Three hours," I repeated, thinking out loud. "So I have one day off a week from work. If I travel to Tenctah, see you, then come back again, that's six hours of the day."

"With the money…"

Ah. I shook my head vehemently. "No, I'm not quitting. I mean, money is great. It's very nice of you. I just really do *like* my job." I bit at my lip. "But I could ask for more days off. I'll talk with Ray about changing my schedule." Ray was basically my second dad; I was sure he'd be able to work it out.

"Good," he said with a quick nod. "I wanted you to be in comfort, when you are not here."

"Three million dollars is an awful lot of money."

"Is it?" he said. "She picked the figure." Behind him, I saw Joanna's colors shift in a way where I knew he was telling the truth. And still I almost said something like, *I just wouldn't want to feel indebted…* But then, too, I thought about gemstone necklaces conjured from thin air, and sprawling alien nations, and princes who had simply no conception of what three million dollars means to your average earthling, and I thought, *maybe let's just say thank you.*

"Thank you," I said.

"What else would you like to know?" Del asked me. I was struck by the sudden realization that he was nervous. Del— nervous! That was a rare sight. But it must mean he wanted this as much as I did. A pleasant warmth bloomed in my chest.

"What about Jexrah and Meervit and—and the rest of your family… your mother and the court…? What will any of them know about this?"

"Nothing initially. I was thinking it would be important for you first to travel to Tenctah and see it in person. I told you we own a residence that's very secluded." His eyes flicked towards me. "We could start there?"

"That sounds like a good plan. Of course your family will find out about us dating eventually." Lord, what a strange conversation this was. But vitally important.

"Yes, they will," he said gravely. Well, we would cross that bridge when we came to it. "And your father will also find out…"

By this point, my dad might have already put all the pieces together. I really had to get home soon. "Let's start with a visit to Tenctah," I said. No need to spend too much of the present on what-ifs. Because who knew what might happen? Could be Del revealed himself to be a royal ass—maybe he was one of those awful people who don't tip their waitstaff or something. Whatever the rumae equivalent of that was.

It wasn't like I was about to walk down the aisle with him. We were just dating.

Which brought me to another thought. "In whatever way we can manage it, I want to go on real dates. The sim room is…" I shuddered. "I need a break from simulations." And yet…

I reached my hand toward him, which he enfolded in his own much larger one. That gave me courage for what I needed to say next. "Del, I need you to tell me why you came to Earth. And what you've been doing while you're here. Please."

His hand tightened a little around mine. Silence enveloped us.

"I won't judge you for whatever it is," I said. *Please tell me. Please trust me.*

"Of course," he started slowly, "much of my time here has been spent attending to my usual duties."

I said a fleeting prayer of sorts. Not another word of this conversation mattered if he couldn't confide in me at last.

"But…" he continued, and I could breathe again. "But I have also been… making use of the sim room to— Recently someone I knew well lost their life. My fault."

"It can't have been your f—"

"It was." He was stony-faced. "It—personal hubris. A series of errors, all on my part." He turned to me. "Did my sister tell you…?"

"Meervit told me the basic facts. She really cares about you,

you know. Jexrah does, too." And perhaps the both of them had conspired to murder me, or maybe just one or the other, but it was all just conjecture—nothing to delve into this very moment.

Del bowed his head. "My errors… my *choices*… I thought to use the sim room to give myself another chance. I ordered Joanna to recreate the key moments that had led to his death. She was greatly upset. Adamant that it was the wrong thing to do." But, of course, Joanna had no choice but to obey. "I thought if the simulation ended with the same result… what use was I to rule? If I couldn't save this person I regarded so highly, then surely… Ailopt—so many people—whatever merits I possessed would never be enough to shoulder the responsibility."

I went cold. "You were testing yourself."

"Yes."

The implications of his words were still sinking in. When Meervit had told me what had happened, she'd revealed her brother had been on Earth for three months. *Three months!* "Oh, Del." I hugged him close. "How many times did you run the simulation?" How many times had he watched his guard die?

"Many," he said. "As many times as I could bear it. The first few times, Joanna had crafted the simulation in such a way that would provide a positive result. I was furious. I had her adjust some details. Then… it became clear that my mind was the enemy. My knowledge of what had actually happened was affecting my actions in the simulation. I had her boost the room's gas levels."

"So that you would forget that all that had already happened," I said. "So that you would react in the moment." My heart was breaking for him—this poor man, mired in a curse of his own creation.

"Yes." His eyes were fixed ahead of him, on a sight only he could see. "Sometimes he lived. Sometimes he did not. When you first arrived on the ship, it was a welcome distraction. The compulsion to run the simulation subsided a little. Then you left, and…" He said no more.

We sat side by side there on the bed. I still had my arms around him, and I wondered how that felt from his perspective. Does an oak tree feel comfort to have his nymph beside him? Or does his tree self, with his thick, knobbled bark, barely register her presence?

"I want to tell you about how my mom died," I said finally.

Del shifted a bit, surprised. "A vehicular accident, you'd said."

"That's right. It happened when I was a little kid. I was in the car—just me in the back seat and her driving up front. It was nighttime, and a deer—that's a larger sort of animal—ran in front of the car. Deer travel together, so we actually avoided the first one. We hit the second one, though. It went right through the windshield. She died pretty much instantly."

I exhaled, trying to slough off the sick feeling I still got when thinking back to that night. So many years later and I still remembered the jumbled terror of the crash, then the terrible silence that had followed. "We'd been driving on a back road. It took a few minutes before someone came along and found us. So there was a bit of time when it was just the two of us, and I—I wasn't so young that I couldn't keep a hold of what had happened. The sequence of events. I'd asked her to change the song on the radio, and she'd reached to do it, then we hit the deer. That stuck in my mind: the radio, her reaching out, the crash. One, two, three. And if she hadn't reached for the radio, then who knows? Then later that same sort of idea… ballooned outward. If I hadn't done this or that before we'd gotten in the car, then we could've missed the deer by a few seconds. So I blamed myself for her death, for a long, long time." I'd never told anyone this, and I wasn't sure anyone had guessed it. Dad, of course, had been dealing with his own loss after Mom's death, and I don't think it had been clear that guilt tinged my grief. The guilt had been something I'd hidden inside, a secret, poisonous kernel, and it had sucked away at me like a black hole swallows light. But then…

"What helped?" Del asked gruffly.

"I started thinking about the person she'd been, instead of just thinking about what had happened. There was a day I got out all our pictures of her and just… looked. She was always smiling, in every single picture. That helped me think about if she'd have wanted me to be torturing myself like that—and the answer was obviously no. She'd have wanted me to be happy. Distraction helped, too. Gardening. And she'd loved our garden, so that… I was honoring her, in a way."

I laid my head against his shoulder. I should be cold, still towel-clad as I was, but his presence beside me was keeping me warm. "I don't want to see the simulation," I said. "I think you should delete it. And you don't even have to tell me any more about what happened. I mean, you can if you want to." I hoped he would. "I just… I trust that you're a good person. And that you'll be a great khinahar. That seems pretty obvious to me. And if you have any doubts about it, think about everyone around you who clearly think otherwise. Your sisters and Joanna. Me. And the person who died, too; I'm sure he'd say the same."

Del was quiet for a minute. I prayed that whatever I'd told him amounted to something worthwhile.

Then, finally, he said, "He was my guard. Also my... you might say a mentor. He went by the name Griva."

"Would you tell me something about him?"

Another pause as he thought. "All the court politicking annoyed him, though there was always much of that. Griva put up with it, for the sake of the position. He... he liked nature best, and he taught me much about it. It was a balm to his life in the city." I remembered Del's practiced ease at lighting the fire, after we'd fallen down the waterfall. Ah.

"I will delete the simulation," he said, and a knot in my chest loosened. He immediately gave Joanna the official order, and I did a little inward dance. Then he asked her the time, and I didn't feel like dancing anymore. About two thirty, Earth time. The day was wearing on, and I didn't want to go. Del made a sort of shifting movement that I knew meant he felt the same.

I drew in a breath, ready (if not thrilled) to discuss practicalities, when—

"Would you ride out with me?" he asked. "Over the mountains?"

"Ride out with you?"

"Yes. I have a craft much like the escape pods. It accommodates two. I thought we could ride out together, just for a while. It might serve to… honor him, as you say. Griva would have liked the sight of your mountains. And then I can return you home."

"Yes," I said. No hesitation. Because there was the matter of my dad and Joe's truck and Joe's poor, wrecked body—these many great, unwieldy messes that I needed to square away, and soon. This next span of time on Earth likely wouldn't be pleasant—probably would be downright *un*pleasant, if I was being honest with myself. I would need to do a stellar job keeping my lies straight. Maybe Joanna could be a help with that.

Yet I wasn't on Earth right now, from a technical standpoint, but floating just above, and that distance, along with the need of the man beside me, put all those concerns temporarily to rest.

It seemed to me, too, that I might be an earthling… but that I was also flirting with something beyond that. "Earthling-plus." Maybe the ambassador designation wasn't so far wrong. And that thought strangely made the decision easy as well.

So I told him yes, then I went to get dressed in the same soft gray catsuit I'd worn the night of the aurora; it was still in the armoire, along with the rest of my fabricated clothes. We'd bring the helmets along, Del said, but no need to wear them unless an emergency presented itself. I liked that; it hinted at a smooth ride and less space between us.

Joanna made Del an outfit to match, and I got to enjoy the treat of watching him undress to get into it. I had to think I was a lucky woman—and time would tell exactly how lucky.

He finished putting on the suit, then turned to me. "Are you ready?"

Just dating.

I nodded and slipped my hand into his.

A MONTANA GIRL
IN A FAR-OUT
WORLD

BEAUTY AND HER ALIEN BOOK THREE
ASCENDED
KATIE JANE GALLAGHER

HIDDEN
BOWER

Thank you so much for reading *Starcrossed*! If you enjoyed this book and have a spare moment, I'd love it if you would write a review on Goodreads or wherever you bought the book. Reviews are key to helping new readers discover my books. Also, if you want to be notified about new releases, sign up for my newsletter at katiejgallagher.com or follow me on Amazon or Facebook!

And again, thank you so much for spending time with my book! That means the entire world to me.

All the best,
Katie

Acknowledgments

I am incredibly grateful to everyone around me who has supported me in making this series a reality. Writing books is like running a marathon, and it would never be possible without the amazing people in my life.

An enormous, wholehearted thank you to my readers for your enthusiasm and support. It is incredible to know that there are people all around the world reading and enjoying my books. More to come!

Many thanks to Tanya Chris, for being my bestest writing buddy along the way, and to Sammy, for providing us his invaluable feline assistance whenever we've written together these past years.

Thank you also to my NaNo CT North crew: Marina Black, Chelsea, Auny, Kat, and everybody else.

Thanks also to Joanna Penn, for giving her blessing for Joanna to remain the character that she is. Yes, perhaps Joanna will take over the world—only time will tell!

Serious thanks to LianaM at 99designs for her incredible cover designs. The work you do is magical—no other word for it.

Thank you to all the writers out there who have crafted iterations of this tale. There are many, *many* versions of Beauty and the Beast, and I read as many retellings as I could get my hands on during the drafting of this series for inspiration.

Thanks and remembrance to Rhapsody, who served as inspiration for Midge and passed during the writing of this series. You are so missed.

To my parents, sister, grandparents, and everyone else in my family, many, many thanks. A shoutout especially to my mom for serving as my gardening expert and fielding all my weird plant questions. I am not a gardener, and somehow I have crafted a story that revolves heavily around plants (huge facepalm).

And, most importantly, thank you to my husband, John. Were it not for your excellent and unflinching advice, Corinne's story would be half of what it is today.

KATIE JANE GALLAGHER is the author of BBNYA finalist *Specter*, the *Beauty and Her Alien* series, and *The Gold in the Dark*. She was born and raised in Illinois, and the magical Naperville Public Library was her home away from home until she ventured to the East Coast for college. Katie graduated magna cum laude from Connecticut College with a BA in Chinese language and literature. She currently lives in Connecticut with her stupendous, half-human half-neanderthal husband and their dopey boxer dog.

To stay updated about upcoming books in the *Beauty and Her Alien* series, as well as other new releases, subscribe to her newsletter at:

KATIEJGALLAGHER.COM